EDGE OF PASSION

DARK REALMS SERIES
BOOK 2

Kathy Kulig

Burnt Stilettos Press
EASTON, PENNSYLVANIA

**Burnt Stilettos
Press**

Kathy Kulig/Burnt Stilettos Press
kathy@kathykulig.com
http://www.BurntStilettosPress.com

Publisher's Note: This is a work of fiction. Names, characters, places,
and incidents are a product of the author's imagination. Locales and
public names are sometimes used for atmospheric purposes. Any
resemblance to actual people, living or dead, or to businesses,
companies, events, institutions, or locales is completely coincidental.
Cover art by Dar Albert
Editing by Bobbie Lyles and Berengaria Brown0

Edge of Passion/ Kathy Kulig. -- 1st ed.
ISBN 978-0-9903439-5-0

"I believe the future is only the past again, entered through another gate.

—ARTHUR WING PINERO

Contents

CHAPTER ONE

Castle Dungeon

"The park's closed today," the gray-haired gentleman at the visitor's desk said in a slow Irish drawl. He scowled at his computer screen then scribbled notes on a piece of paper without looking at her.

"I'm not a tourist, I'm Dana Brennan. I was hired as a musician for the show."

Glancing up from his work, he gave her a quick once-over and frowned. "What happened to you, miss? You're soaking wet." He stood and approached the counter from the other side, giving her a closer look. "Didn't fall into the bog now, did you?"

"Bog? No, I had a flat tire on my drive over. It was raining."

"Changed it yourself now?"

She nodded.

He smiled, clearly astonished. He was a man of indeterminate years with white hair, a weatherworn face and blue eyes that held humor one moment, and severity the next.

"I'll get you your key so you can get into dry clothes. I'm Will Donegal, the proprietor of Rathmoor Castle." He opened several drawers until he held up a key. "Here you go, Ms. Brennan. Take the road to the right of the castle. You'll find the cottages for the performers." He handed her the key with the number six on it. "You be an American? First time in Ireland?"

"I am American, but I've visited before. My cousin lives in Dublin. She told me about the job."

"I'd come and show you the cottage, but I best be staying here. Being it's Monday, the park is closed, but tourists still wander in."

Her spirits fell. "Darn. I was hoping to check out the castle. It looks magnificent from the outside."

"It is that now, isn't it?" His eyes brightened and his back straightened, then he turned serious again. "You'll have plenty of time to explore the castle when it's open."

"I will. Thanks." She sighed. "I'm supposed to meet Jack. I understand he's the one who hired me." They'd talked on the phone and emailed for months. She had all the music he'd sent her memorized for the show. She couldn't wait to meet him. Curiosity stirred that fluttery sensation in her stomach.

She couldn't help but wonder if his looks matched her fantasy image of him. At the same time, she worried if she didn't perform well, Jack had the power to fire her, and this exciting summer job and vacation would abruptly end.

His voice had a slow, rugged sound. Maybe it was the Irish accent or her pitiful love life that had kicked her libido into gear. She hadn't had anything more than a casual date over the last six months. Knowing her luck, Jack probably looked more like the proprietor.

"Jack's around," Mr. Donegal said. "His cottage is at the edge of the forest, number two. And best you don't wander into that forest alone. You could get lost in the bogs."

"I'll keep that in mind." Get lost? She used to go backpacking in the Shenandoah National Park alone and she never got lost. She thought better not to mention that. "I had a large package shipped. Do you know if it's arrived yet?"

He pondered her question for a moment. "Yes, it's here. Delivered two days ago."

"Where is it? How did it look?" She clasped her hands to her chest, preparing herself for the worse.

He gave her a puzzled look. "Why, it looked like a box, a rather large one at that."

"I mean was it damaged?

"Don't think so."

"Good. Can I pick it up now, please?"

"Jack took it. Said it was your harp. Probably took it to the castle for the show."

"And the castle is closed," she reminded him. Her heart leapt with relief and disappointment. By the look on the proprietor's face, he wasn't going to leave his post so she could get her instrument.

"Ah, I love the folk harp. 'Tis a lovely sound. I shall look forward to hearing you play."

"Thank you, Mr. Donegal."

He caught her gaze and gave her a slight nod. "If you follow the drive, you'll come to a fork. Bear to the right. You'll see the cottages. There's a meeting tonight at seven in the castle for the entertainers. You can get your harp then."

She thanked him again and left the visitor's center with its quaint thatched roof and miniature windows with flower boxes, like something straight out of a fairytale. Despite her disappointment in having to wait to practice her music, her summer job excited her. Her parents had frowned on Dana's decision to take a leave of absence from a well-paying management position in a security company for this part-time, minimal-paying job as an entertainer in a medieval show.

Both high-powered executives, they thrived on long work hours and stress. How could they understand that the stress of Dana's job had been wearing on her life?

Work usually slowed down in her company over the summer, so her boss had agreed to the leave as long as she returned by September first. She deserved this break. At thirty-three, this was the first reckless thing she'd ever done.

The midday sun dried the earlier rain and the air smelled of dew, cut grass and flowers. For a Maryland girl, June in Ireland was on the cool side. She climbed into her rental car, which looked more like a fishbowl on a roller skate, and drove along the gravel road toward Rathmoor Castle. As she reached the fork in the road, she stopped the car. Across a large field toward the right, a dozen thatched-roofed cottages lined the edge of a dense forest. The left fork led straight to the castle. The ancient castle stood in the center of a large meadow. The worn stone edifice conveyed power and strength. The centuries hadn't diminished that.

As she gazed at the massive structure, a slight tremor went through her. Mostly, she shivered from cold. The rain had soaked through to her underwear and the cool air had chilled her to the bone. But the tremor was more than that. She couldn't imagine her good luck at working in such a beautiful place, but what if her parents were right and taking this time off would somehow hurt her position at her old job? She drew in a breath as a sudden case of nerves overwhelmed her with doubt. As much as she loved the adventurous nature of her summer job, was she being practical?

She found herself hoping to go back to her old routine as soon as possible. Why did she think she could make a big change in her life? Fulfill a life-long dream as a musician. That wasn't her.

Dana swung the car toward the cottages and stopped in front of number six. After unloading her luggage, she dragged it all into her unit and dropped it on the bed. The cottage was small but very neat. A tiny kitchen with a table for two was at the front, a bed and dresser in the middle, then a seating area with loveseat and coffee table. A stone fireplace took over one wall. Her teeth chattered and a hot shower beckoned.

She showered and changed into jeans and a tee shirt and slipped on a lightweight hooded sweatshirt, leaving it unzipped. Grabbing her room key and stuffing it in her sweatshirt pocket, she gave her unpacked suitcases a weary look as she left her cottage.

When she tried Jack's door and got no answer, she accepted the grim fact that harp practice would have to wait until after the meeting that evening. The castle loomed in front of her and begged exploration. A drive into town for groceries would wait. How could she pass up scouting the grounds of a five-hundred-year-old monument? Closed or not, she had to take a closer look. She had all afternoon to shop and unpack. As she climbed the hill toward the castle, she admired how the dark stone structure rose well above the trees and at each corner were tower-like turrets. The view from the top must be amazing.

After working in a security company for thirteen years, force of habit had her scanning the castle walls for security cameras or spotlights. No cameras, minimal lighting, no motion sensors. She hoped the park had a better system in place inside, considering the castle was supposed to have fifteenth- and sixteenth-century furnishings.

Why did the castle have to be closed today? Just her luck. She walked up the drawbridge and tried the door and found it locked. Crap. Maybe it wasn't so easy to break into a castle.

Walking around the building, she ran her hand along the rough stone. Five hundred years old. She tried to imagine what it would've been like to live here centuries ago. The sophisticated lords and ladies must have had many lavish feasts and celebrations. And all summer she would be entertaining in this beautiful, historical place. A dream come true. She couldn't contain her smile.

She hadn't practiced in over two weeks since she'd shipped her harp. Even though the audiences for the dinner shows would be small, her stomach knotted as if she was about to perform at a huge symphony hall.

Three-quarters around the building, she discovered a small alcove and a wooden service door at the end of the narrow walkway. Dana tugged on the metal door latch and it opened. She shook her head. Very poor security. She should mention this to Jack and make some recommendations while she was here.

A narrow-curved stairway led up. She preferred to learn the layout of the place before she started work, since the first show would be in a couple of days. One flight up opened onto a great hall. A few tapestries hung on the walls between giant windows and heavy dark chairs and one table nearly took up the entire room. They'd need more tables to seat guests. There must be another room.

Dana crossed the hall to another doorway that led to a different stairway and was about to climb, when she saw a flickering glow from the darkness below. Fire? Could the castle be on fire? Wiring or the furnishings could be. She trotted down the circular stone stairs.

CHAPTER TWO

Voyeur

Darkness crept in around her except for the golden, flickering light from the basement. Walking through another doorway, she thought she heard voices but she wasn't sure. The hairs on the back of her neck stood up.

As she rounded a stone partition, the room brightened. Flames flickered within a half dozen wrought-iron sconces; a fire burned in a small stone fireplace. The room smelled of sweet burning wood and damp stone. At the far wall two people hovered in shadows. Dana remained in her circle of darkness at the bottom of the stairs, unable to tear her gaze away from the frightening sight.

A naked woman, suspended from the ceiling, was bound with straps. Her wrists and ankles secured and spread wide in a V shape. Torn between wanting to rush over to rescue her, or run out and call for help, Dana froze. She couldn't move or speak.

A narrow hammock cradled and supported the woman's back and bottom. Her pussy and anus lay open wide, and metal clamps were attached to her nipples. Dana winced at the distended tips protruding from the tight clamps. The woman also wore a blindfold. The other person, a male, wore a hooded robe. His back faced Dana.

A rush of heat, then cold crept through her. Wrapping her arms around her waist, her first instinct was to escape and call for help. Then she stepped back and searched for a weapon, planning to do some damage to the guy if the woman needed help. Instead, Dana froze at the bottom of the stairs. Attacking this man was not a good idea if the woman was a willing participant. She would watch long enough to make sure the woman was okay.

There were people who got into this kinky stuff. Why would this woman allow this man to do these things? "More, slave?" the man in the robe asked the woman.

The woman nodded. "Yes, Master, if it pleases you." His fingers stroked the narrow thatch of dark hair between her legs, avoiding the glistening folds of her pussy. The woman squirmed and tried lifting her hips.

Dana managed to breathe in teaspoon-sized portions of air. People did this for fun? It didn't look like fun. Was the woman in trouble? Should she stop this? Go for help? Move, dammit.

"You want me to touch your clit, don't you?"

The woman whimpered and arched her back. "Yes, Sir."

"But I hadn't given you permission to move." He continued to tease her, his fingers trailing along her inner thighs, across her ass and back to the thatch of hair.

The woman moaned in pleasure. "No, Sir. You didn't. I forgot."

His hand moved to her breasts and adjusted the nipple clamps until she let out a little yelp and sharp intake of breath. "I'll have to punish you for forgetting."

"Yes, Sir."

He swung a flogger in the air several times. The woman's chest rose and fell quickly as if anticipating the blows that would come. Dana held her breath. The robed man struck her ass and she cried out and jerked against her bindings. Her feet pointed and her legs tried to spread wider.

"Yes, Master, again. Please."

Biting her lip, Dana clamped a hand over her mouth. Good lord, the woman enjoyed this.

"Not just yet. You're being an insolent slave today." He chuckled as the flogger swatted her bottom and the underside of her thighs.

Dana's blood chilled with the sharp crack of leather hitting the woman's bare skin. As he hit her again and again, the woman slumped in her restraints, her head hung to one side. He approached her and brushed her long dark hair from her face and kissed her forehead tenderly. Whimpering, the woman leaned into the kiss. Dana stared at the couple shamelessly. She should leave quietly but couldn't pull herself away.

"Good," he said. "You ready for more?"

The woman nodded and leaned into his hand. He walked over to the wall and pulled an object out of a tote bag then came back to the woman.

"You remember the safe signals with a gag?"

"Yes, Master. Three quick grunts or open and close my hands."

"Yes." He bent down to kiss her. "Now open." A ball gag was secured in her mouth. He tied the straps around the back of her head. Now the woman couldn't scream if she needed to.

Dana couldn't shout or run. Should she trust this man or do something?

"You're such a pain slut, my love." The man stroked her hair then he swung the flogger in a circle. Turning to the side, the man faced Dana. His robe gaped open, and he was naked underneath. His hard cock jutted out from the draped fabric. "I think you like pain as much as coming."

The woman made a mewling sound as she nodded.

"You want to come, don't you?" His hand slipped between her legs, then he plunged a finger inside her.

She nodded and moaned, trying to raise her hips.

"No, stay," he ordered, pulling his hand away. He then swung the flogger and swatted straight across her breasts.

The woman gave a yelp as much as she could with a gag in her mouth.

Dana bit her lip as heat flowed through her followed by a throbbing in her pussy. Lord, she was wet and getting turned on by this. The man lapped at the woman's clamped nipples, then took a swollen tip between his teeth. The woman jerked against her restraints. "Too painful?" he asked.

She shook her head and arched her back, offering her breasts to him. He bit harder this time and the woman cried out beneath the gag. Dana's nipples hardened too and her pussy was sopping. How could the woman stand that kind of torture and appear to beg for more?

"Are you ready to be fucked?" he asked as his hand dipped down to her slit.

She nodded, writhing in her restraints.

"I'm going to fuck you, but I want to taste you first."

The woman let out a groan and looked at her right hand. She had her pinky finger extended. He looked up. "You're signaling you're on the edge?"

She nodded.

"Good. I'll go slowly." He cracked the flogger in the air. The sound made the woman and Dana jump. "But don't come until I give you permission. I still wish to taste you so you must remain in control."

The woman nodded slightly and whimpered. Stroking her breasts, the man then moved his hand lower, circling her pussy. His mouth positioned between her legs and Dana could see he blew across her clit and labia. The woman groaned. Dana held her hand over her mouth.

Obviously, these were lovers, strange as it was, and she needed to get out of there before they saw her. Slowly, she took a step back and another, but somehow managed to trip over her own feet in the darkness. Stumbling, she fell back against the wall. The movement and noise caught the man's attention. He jerked his head toward Dana and gave her a narrowed look.

CHAPTER THREE

Temptation

"**Y**ou going to explain what the hell you're doing?" The man in the robe took several steps closer, the flogger still gripped in his right hand. The folds of his robe opened and he didn't make any move to hide his cock. Sliding the hood back off his head, he let the robe hang off his shoulders, giving her a view of his face and body. Straight black hair fell past his shoulders. Dark, intense eyes lingered on her breasts, then he locked his gaze with hers. His stern frown eased into an intimidating smile. "You like to watch, I can tell."

The woman hanging from the straps struggled against her restraints and moaned.

"It's all right. We have a visitor, my love, but I don't think she means any harm." He studied Dana. "Do you?"

Dana shook her head. "No. I saw a light. I thought it might be a fire." As if that explained her presence in the castle when it was closed to the public.

"Except you pulled my lady out of her sub space." His smile was grim and tone annoyed. "Never interrupt a session."

She wasn't sure what he meant. "I didn't mean to disturb you. I wanted to make sure…" She was going to say make sure the woman wasn't tied up against her will, but she'd figured that out the first minute. Then why hadn't she left sooner?

"That something ominous wasn't going on here?" He laughed. "I can see your nipples through the bra. You like to watch. It's in your eyes too. You're turned on. Maybe you'd like to be next?"

Dana swallowed and took a step back.

He laughed. "Another time perhaps. You can stay if you wish. My lady likes to be watched. But you cannot interfere and you must remove your clothes."

Her pussy throbbed painfully at the thought of his suggestion. She'd soaked through her panties. This was turning her on, and scaring the hell out of her too. How did he know? "I think I'll go. Sorry to disturb you."

He looked annoyed. "Suit yourself."

She backed up the spiral stone steps. As soon as she couldn't see him anymore, she turned and ran the rest of the way. Running across the main hall on the first floor, she found the door to the outside, yanked it open and raced toward the front of the castle where she'd parked her car.

A fine misty rain cooled her heated face but her body burned and ached with a desire she didn't understand. She kept glancing behind her, expecting to see the naked man in the black, hooded robe chasing her. As she came around the front turret, she crashed into him.

Dana screamed and stumbled back. Strong, muscular arms enclosed her.

"Easy now, miss. Are you all right?"

She looked up into calm, blue eyes that held concern, not the intense annoyance of the man in the castle's dungeon. "Let go of me." She pushed at his chest. Despite the cool air, he wore a short-sleeved shirt that showed off decent-sized biceps.

He released her and she took a step back. "You running from a ghost?" the guy asked, smiling. Not the man in the black, hooded robe. He was taller, his hair shorter and he wore jeans, not a robe, thank God.

She held a hand to her chest while she sucked in air, trying to catch her breath. "Who the hell are you? You scared the daylights out of me."

"I'm Jack."

"Jack Murray?"

He nodded, smiling with a glint of mischief in his eyes. "And you are…"

He was much better-looking than she'd imagined him. During months of email she'd made her own fantasy image. Thick, dark hair was combed back but a wavy lock fell low over his brow. He stood a few inches taller than she and appeared to be about the same age. "I'm Dana. I just got here."

"Dana, hello." His eyebrows went up. "Got here. From where?" He gave her an odd look, probably trying to figure out why she ran from behind the castle.

She hesitated. Glancing over her shoulders, she half expected to see the naked guy, robe flowing behind him as he chased after her. Her heart still pounded.

Jack looked past her as if he too expected to see someone.

"Dublin. I drove in from Dublin." She'd rather get far away from the castle right now. What if that guy came out and saw her? But Jack was the one who'd hired her or recommended her for the job. She took a deep breath and let the air out slowly, willing herself to relax. She glanced back again. If the robed guy was chasing her, he would've been out by now.

She turned back and met Jack's eyes and her stomach did a twirl. Actually, he was damn hot, no question there. Heat flamed her face and traveled south making her horny all over again. What was wrong with her? Maybe jet lag. God, she didn't need the inconvenience of a summer fling, not that he'd be interested. Even if he was, it wasn't worth the trouble or pain. She imagined the awkward moment when she had to return to the states.

"Something wrong?" Jack lifted a brow.

"No, I'm fine."

He studied her for a heart-pounding moment with an intense gaze which made her a bit wobbly on her feet. The corner of his mouth quirked in a grin.

"Did the other harpist have her baby?" she asked.

"Don't think so."

"The job is still mine through the end of August?" Something about Jack was very appealing—the easy way he talked, that Irish accent, the spark in his eyes, and at the same time, unsettling. She wasn't sure if that was a good thing or bad.

In his emails, he'd mentioned he wasn't married, but didn't say if he had a girlfriend. Their chats had occasionally gotten a little personal, but mostly they were business friendly. She glanced at his left hand and confirmed he didn't wear a wedding ring. Not that all men wore wedding bands.

He smiled and she wondered if he caught her checking him out. Her heart gave a little leap. She didn't believe in love at first sight but she did believe in instant attraction. Either the man was charismatic or her hormones were strung out after the bizarre scene she just witnessed.

"Yes, through August." He looked over her shoulder, and she spun around to see what he looked at.

Had the man in the robe finally come out?

"Someone with you?" he asked.

She shook her head. "No, no. Just looking around the castle."

"Ah, 'tis quite a fine, old place. I can show you now if you like."

"No!"

He grinned. "Another time, perhaps."

"Yes, thanks. I should get to my cottage and unpack. I thought I'd drive into town for groceries then take a walk in the forest." She didn't want to ask for her harp now. Mr. Donegal had said it was in the castle.

"Lots of bogs in the forest behind the cottages. Careful if you decide to go on that walk. Stay on the trails."

"Thanks for the tip," she said with a hint of sarcasm. Did they think she was from the city and never took a walk in the woods?

"You'll be wanting your harp?" he asked.

Dana panicked. She wanted to say yes, but she didn't want to go back inside the castle.

"I'll bring it to you. It's in my cottage."

CHAPTER FOUR

Sensual Harp

After Jack brought Dana's harp to her cottage, he drove into town to work at his uncle's clothing store. Later, as he crossed the meadow toward home, haunting harp music drifted from Dana's place. The melody he recognized as one of the songs from the show. He stood on the gravel walkway in front of her porch mesmerized by the smooth precision of her music and the sensual flow of the notes. An accomplished player, not an amateur.

Her beauty equaled her music. She should be performing in a large symphony orchestra, not a small medieval dinner show.

While he listened, the stress of the afternoon eased from his shoulders. It had been a disappointing day. Another loan application turned down. He was running out of options. The thought of returning to his old job in the wool mills didn't appeal to him. The last seven years he'd been running his uncle's store, pulled it out of near bankruptcy and now his uncle planned to sell it. The money from the sale would be his uncle's retirement. If Jack was the new owner, his uncle could continue to work part-time. But if Jack couldn't get a loan to buy the store, his uncle would be forced to look for another buyer and would lose his part-time job. His uncle couldn't afford to hold a loan for Jack.

The music stopped and Jack held his breath in the still afternoon. Was his private concert over? He wondered why she would come all the way to Ireland for a summer job. Nothing in their emails had given him a clue as to why.

The music began again, a difficult classical piece for as much as he knew about music, not part of the show. He was a singer, not a musician. He closed his eyes, lost in his private performance. His mind wandered and easily imagined Dana playing the harp naked, then incorporating a pattern of rope bondage for that scene, allowing only her hands and arms free to play. He would slowly release her unbridled sensuality. Tension and sexual heat built when a sub's trust relinquished control to him. That always pleasured him the most.

Someone that skilled at an instrument had to be regimented and disciplined, a master of her harp. Had she ever allowed anyone to Master her in the bedroom?

Dana reminded him of a sub he once knew at Dagda's Edge. Cleona never fit in with the other guests of the cottage. She craved release, and Jack thought he could reach her. At times she responded to his commands and explored her deepest desires. But her tormented past and those bonds of insecurity and guilt threw up walls he couldn't conquer. She hesitated with whatever measures he tried, and he knew when not to push her boundaries. She was out of place and inexperienced with BDSM.

Every guest of the cottage, or Dagda's Edge, had to be invited. He didn't quite understand the mystery or science behind the cottage other than it had been built centuries ago on the intersections of ley lines, and the electromagnetic energy had the power to transmute time and dimensions.

He didn't understand it, nor did most of the guests. They just accepted it. Dru, the manager, seemed to understand. He wasn't sure where she originated from, and wondered if she had the ability to control the energy surrounding the cottage. She always denied she had that gift.

Jack first met Cleona at Dagda's Edge. Adara, the cottage's bartender, had introduced them. The two women were friends. It didn't take long for Jack to realize both women were not from the area, although they claimed to be from Ireland. At the time, he had no idea how displaced they were.

Cleona had been a willing submissive at first, but Jack wasn't prepared for the doubts and fears she struggled with.

He knew she had been in a relationship with another man, engaged perhaps, but Cleona refused to talk about it. He believed Adara, had guided Cleona into the forest, to Dagda's Edge, as a means to escape her lover's control.

Maybe it was Jack's inability to meet her needs, to gain her trust, or perhaps Cleona felt guilt, didn't like this foreign land, or didn't want to give up her vanilla lifestyle. She chose to leave Dagda's Edge and return to her home and lover. A painful and tearful choice. Painful for him as well.

Jack had learned his lesson. Never bring an inexperienced submissive to Dagda's Edge. He needed to keep Dana out of the forest and away from the cottage.

If they had more time, perhaps, he could bring her around slowly.

He suspected her normal life was usually focused and in control. But under the careful attentions of a Dom, would she surrender her sensual side and completely let go? During their many chats online, he wondered if Dana had picked up on his Dom nature. At first emails were business related, discussing the dinner show, its production and where she'd be living, then progressed to friendly teasing and a little suggestive chat.

He said things like, 'I'll instruct you on what will be required as my harpist.' And she replied, 'I'll do everything I can to meet your needs.' He could have mistaken her outgoing American nature for blatant flirting.

His cock hungered for the opportunity to train a sub, to have her surrender her physical self to him. There was something very enticing about bringing a novice into the lifestyle. She'd either be curious enough to ease into it or be scared off. Jack couldn't deny who he was—a sexual Dominant looking for a woman willing to take on the role as his submissive. But the downside was choosing a sub not ready for the extreme tastes and desires of a master. Did he want to put himself through all that again?

Unfortunately, the troupe couldn't afford to be without a harpist. His priority was to help Donegal, the owner, find a temporary harpist, to replace Jane while she had her babe, not find a new slave for himself. The summer was their busiest season and he didn't have time to hire and train someone new.

"Taking a nap are you, Jack?"

Jack shook himself out of his musing, opened his eyes and looked at Damon. The fellow troupe member and friend studied him with devilish dark eyes. "Nah, listening to the new girl play. She's good, isn't she?" Jack answered.

Damon, the violinist, tilted his head toward Dana's cottage. His long dark hair was damp, and a large duffel slung over his shoulder. "Yeah, she is that. Is she coming to the meeting tonight? She needs to get her costume," Damon said.

"I don't know. She didn't say."

"You met her then. Is she cute?"

"Very." Jack couldn't stop himself from smiling.

"Ah, Jack. I know that look. You'll be wanting to tie her up and do unmentionable things to her." Damon narrowed his eyes. "But don't scare her off now. We need a harpist for the summer."

"I know," Jack groaned. He could listen to her play all day.

"You could go to Dagda's Edge and find a willing lady."

Jack shrugged. "For the night, yes, but I want more. A woman in my life, not just a one-night partner. I'd like what you and Shannon have."

Damon nodded. "I understand. Shannon and I are going to get something to eat before the meeting. Want to join us?"

"I'll pass, thanks. I think I'll check on the harpist." He gave Damon a wink.

* * *

"Dinner?" Jack asked, an easy smile greeting her at the opened doorway to her cottage.

"Jack! Hi." Dana's stomach gave a bit of a flutter. She knew he was probably looking at her opened suitcases with clothes piled all over the bed. Once she'd had her harp, she'd given up unpacking to practice. It'd been over two weeks since she'd played. Usually if she went more than a day she started climbing the walls. "What?" Sometimes when she played her harp she'd get so disconnected from the world. It took her a second to understand what he asked. "A little early for dinner, isn't it? I was going to find a market in town for groceries. I can cook something here."

His eyebrows rose. "It's twenty minutes to town. I doubt you'll have time if you plan to make the meeting."

"I have all afternoon." She checked her watch. It was nearly five p.m. "Oh my God. I was playing for four hours." She suddenly realized she was hungry. "I guess I'll have to go after the meeting."

Jack shook his head. "Bet you didn't have lunch either."

She didn't answer.

"Follow me," he ordered, walking off her porch, not waiting for her to answer.

"Hang on, let me get my sweatshirt." Dana sorted through the clothes on her bed and found her sweatshirt and put it on. She slipped the room key in her pocket and felt an object like a large coin. She pulled it out and studied it. Not a coin, but the intricate detail of an old brooch. Made of either bronze or copper, a coiled design like a labyrinth circle sat in the center surrounded by Celtic knots.

Weird. She didn't remember anyone giving her the brooch, and wondered if it was an artifact and maybe she could be in trouble for having it. She turned it over and found nothing carved on the back. The idea that someone must've slipped it in her pocket was unsettling and a little annoying.

"Dana?" Jack called from her porch.

"Coming." She placed the brooch in a drawer and planned to take it back to the castle later, then rushed out of her cottage, locked her door, and ran to catch up to him.

CHAPTER FIVE

Cloaked Figures

"Where are we going?" she asked Jack.

He didn't answer and kept walking. She hesitated for a moment then decided to see what he had in mind. Jack had to go to the meeting too. Maybe he knew a local place where she could get a quick bite.

"Are you going to tell me where we're going?"

"Jack's place."

"And why are we going to your place?" she asked. He gave her a sexy grin and her pulse kicked up a few beats. The sexy voice she remembered hearing on the phone certainly matched the rugged good looks of the man before her. Following him gave her a nice view of him from the back, from wide shoulders, to the tight ass in snug jeans to boots.

He glanced over his shoulder and shot her a dark look from blue-gray eyes. "Trust me." His cottage had the same layout as hers—the kitchenette at the front of the cottage, the bed with a red patterned duvet and a loveseat in the back. It was neat and organized except for several boxes stacked in one corner, a laptop computer on the small dining table and a bicycle propped against a wall. A wide window overlooked the forest behind the cottages.

In the kitchenette, he took out pots and pans, sliced brown bread and removed an enormous amount of food from the refrigerator.

"I don't want you to go to any trouble," she said.

"Shepherd's Pie is no trouble. It's dinner. Have a seat. It won't take long. But this kitchen is too small for two people." He handed her silverware and pointed to one of two chairs at the small dining table. After fixing them both a cup of tea, he went to work on their meal.

"Thanks, Jack." She watched him boil the potatoes and prepare a meat filling. As he added rosemary, thyme and other spices to the bubbling mixture, Dana inhaled the savory aroma. "Mmm. That smells wonderful."

"Won't be long." He added the meat and vegetable mixture to a casserole dish and covered it with mashed potatoes, then slid it into the oven.

He sat at the table and poured more tea. "How long have you been playing the harp? Is that your full-time job?"

She tightened the grip around her mug, suddenly reminded the fulfillment of her dream was only temporary. "I've been playing the harp since I was eight years old. I dreamed of playing in a symphony someplace, but my parents felt that dream was not practical so I went to school for electrical engineering and work designing security systems. Not very glamourous but it pays the bills."

He frowned. "Sounds like you don't like it much."

She shrugged. "It's okay."

"Do you get to play your harp in other concerts?"

She stared at the table and grasped her hands in her lap. "No, I play for my own pleasure."

"That's sad."

She looked at him and smiled. "I enjoy playing. I don't need an audience."

He grunted.

"How long have you been doing the show?"

He leaned back with his mug and took a sip. "Couple years. It's a part-time job and doesn't pay much. I also manage my uncle's store. Before the show, I worked in the woolen mills factory. I hated it. I'm trying to buy out my uncle's shop so he can retire. I'm waiting to see if the bank will cooperate. If not, I'll return to the mills."

"I hope it works out for you."

Jack got up and took the casserole out of the oven, served portions on two plates and cut slices of the homemade bread. "How do you like it? Good?" he asked after she'd tasted it.

"This is great. You didn't bake the bread, did you?"

He laughed. "No. I'll take you to the market in the morning and show you around town, including the bakery."

"That's really nice of you." She glanced around his cottage. "What do you sell at your uncle's store?" She devoured the shepherd's pie. Have to love a guy who could cook.

"Woolens and leather goods."

"I'll have to stop by and check it out. I'm sure I could use a sweater in this weather. Ireland's summers are cooler than I'm used to." Something about the way the man looked at her made her squirm in her seat. Not in a bad way. He had the most gorgeous blue eyes, sensual, intense but at the same time calming. "Not the season for leather though. Too warm and too much rain."

Jack smiled. "Leather never goes out of season." The look he gave her spread heat and longing through her. It was a very bad idea to get involved with someone considering she would leave in three months. "Leather goods provide our largest sales in the summer." His voice lowered. "Some of our clientele have special requests."

The way he said it made her feel strangely aroused. Her nipples tingled and hardened and her pussy throbbed. "Should I ask?"

He shrugged. "Fetish wear and bondage equipment. More pie?" He got up and spooned another serving of shepherd pie.

She swallowed. "No, thanks. I've had enough."

His gaze locked with hers as if he was testing her, waiting to see if she'd react to the comment about leather goods. This reminded her of a business deal. Was he playing games with her? If he was, she wasn't going to let him rile her. "Interesting. And what's your best-selling SM device?"

Smiling he said, "Floggers, then various restraints. A lot of people enjoy pain."

"Mmmm." She said it in a tone as if they spoke about the weather or a favorite movie.

"What do know of the SM scene?" He was serious, the teasing tone gone.

She took in a breath. Images of the couple in the castle's dungeon flashed in her mind. Heat flowed through her like warmed honey. Her pussy felt wet and achy. "Not a lot. I read some about it. Curious, I guess."

He smiled. "Fantasized then?"

She choked on the last spoonful of her dinner. "Wow, this conversation got personal. From groceries to bondage to sexual fantasies." Her voice shook and her whole body heated. Exhilarated by the topic, she pressed her thighs together as her pussy clenched and pulsed. Damn, this man had her worked up now, and she'd only just met him. "Why didn't you mention this in your emails?"

"You mean about working in a store?"

She laughed nervously. "I mean about the SM products you sell."

He shrugged. "I didn't want to scare you off. We needed a harpist and your cousin highly recommended you."

"I don't scare too easily." She smiled. God, was she flirting? Yes, she was flirting and wasn't he her coworker?

"What does scare you?" He shot her a self-satisfied grin.

Her mind went to the couple in the dungeon. Had they bought leather items from Jack's store? Was she scared by what she'd seen? Or intrigued? This time she shrugged. "I'll have to let you know."

"I'll count on that," he lowered his voice and heat flowed through her. "We should go to the castle."

"What?" she breathed. Dana's heart fluttered as she thought about Jack tying her up in the dungeon. So soon? He didn't waste any time.

"The meeting is starting in a few minutes. What did you think I meant?"

"Nothing."

* * *

After Jack introduced Dana to everyone, he walked her through her parts. Why was she so nervous? She knew the music. She met the other minstrel players, singers and actors.

"Damon and Shannon will be up later. They're bringing the costumes from the dry cleaners," said Jack. "There'll be a rehearsal at three tomorrow. This is mainly for the benefit of our new member, Dana. She knows the music. I've heard her play. She'll do fine in the show tomorrow."

"Tomorrow?" Dana squeaked. She thought she'd have a couple days.

"Is there a problem?" Jack asked.

"No, looking forward to it." She swallowed. Dana glanced at Jack, giving him a worried look. Not much time to practice. Talk about getting thrown to the wolves.

Returning her gaze, he gave her a reassuring smile with a slight nod. He must know what she was thinking. Did she have that panicked look in her eyes?

"You'll be fine," he whispered in her ear.

"That's all I have for you," Jack said. "Any questions?"

Everyone shook their heads. "Except for the costumes," Thea, a woman with long reddish hair said. There were eight people in the troupe, four women and four men, minus the couple who was missing. Thea was the flute player, her boyfriend, Kevin, played the uilleann pipes, which sounded a bit like bagpipes, and two dancers. "I hope it's soon. We all have plans tonight."

Jack nodded. "I know. Hang here for a few. I'll give Dana a quick tour while we wait for Damon and Shannon." He held out his hand, pointing the way to a spiral staircase. "After you."

Dana followed Jack up the shadowed staircase. He pointed out several rooms that had once been bedrooms, a chapel, guest rooms and servant quarters. Then the stairs opened onto the roof. A gust of cool air penetrated her sweatshirt and she shivered. "Wow, what a view."

"You can't see much in the dark. But I wanted to talk to you."

"I'm glad to be here, Jack." She could feel him studying her and the butterflies flitted around in her stomach. "What did you want to talk about?"

She heard him let out a breath. "I want to know what you were so afraid of before. Why were you running from the castle earlier?"

She wanted to tell him, but she was embarrassed and confused by her reaction. She wasn't afraid, not anymore. Mostly she was turned on. How could she tell him this? A previous boyfriend had tied her up a couple times for fun during sex, but it wasn't anything like what she saw in the dungeon. "I can't."

"Don't you trust me?"

She let out a half laugh. "Jack, I don't know you."

"We've been talking for months."

"It's not the same."

"Take the chance. I can be trusted."

The sound of voices far below caught her attention. Dana looked over the stone wall and flood lights from the castle illuminated the entertainers walking across the meadow carrying costumes. Beautiful medieval dresses for the ladies, and doublets and breeches for the guys.

"Shannon and Damon are back," Jack said, looking over the wall. "Maybe you'll tell me later."

Back down the stairs, Dana entered the grand hall again and it was empty. Then at one end she saw two people hunched over the large table with medieval clothing draped on top.

"Hey, you two. What kept you?" Jack asked.

The guy spun around and Dana gasped. "The dry cleaners had a time finding all the costumes—" He took a look at Dana and smiled. "Hello, there." By the way he looked at her, Dana knew he recognized her from the dungeon. "Look who's here, Shannon. Our visitor from earlier." The woman with long, dark hair turned around and gave Dana an up-and-down look, her mouth pressed together as if trying to hold back a smile. Her fingers played at the cleavage of her low-cut sweater.

"Welcome to Rathmoor Castle," Shannon said with a teasing grin. "Next time maybe you'll stay longer or join in?"

"I don't think so. Sorry I disturbed you." Dana couldn't stop herself from remembering Damon naked in the black robe, or Shannon strapped up, legs spread. Her face felt flushed and her nipples tightened.

"Am I missing something?" Jack said.

"You'll have to ask Dana for the details." Damon grinned. The man didn't look embarrassed at all. "My guess is we have a sub smoldering beneath that demure surface. With the right Master—"

Shannon punched him in the arm. "Stop it." She turned to Dana. "Ignore him. He's shameless, but harmless."

Dana glanced toward Jack's questioning look. "I'll tell you later." She wasn't about to go into details in front of this couple.

"She's more beautiful than Cleona," Damon said. "Though she has the same eyes."

Shannon huffed and rolled her eyes. "Damon. She doesn't care about that."

"Who's Cleona?" Dana asked.

"Jack's previous lover," Damon said. "She left several months ago."

Jack's face remained expressionless.

"I think you'll love your costume," Shannon said, obviously trying to change the subject. Picking up a forest-green velvet dress in her arms, she brought it to

Dana. "This should fit you according to the measurements you sent us."

"It's beautiful. Thank you." She glanced at Jack. "I should go and practice. See you all tomorrow."

"Would you like me to walk you back?" Jack's expression turned serious.

"No," she said a little too forcefully. "It's been a long day." That brought a snicker from Shannon and Damon. She didn't acknowledge them, just descended the stairs out of the castle.

Back in her cottage, she hung the dress on a hook on the closet door, then tried playing her harp, but even that didn't help calm her. Images of Shannon and Damon in the dungeon haunted her mind. She could hear the flogger striking Shannon's ass and thighs and see the inflamed flesh, while Damon fondled her exposed nether region. Shannon had appeared to be in ecstasy. Was that type of sex really pleasurable? She'd had a few good lovers but had she ever experienced extreme ecstasy? Would Jack do something like that?

Everywhere her body tingled as she fantasized about standing in the dungeon naked. Jack would restrain her and strike her with the flogger until her skin was red and raw, then stimulate her clit, thrusting his cock inside her. She groaned out loud. Enough, she was torturing herself.

From her sitting area she looked out the window into the forest. Yes, she did have the same view as Jack. Dim light from the cottages illuminated a narrow path that led from the meadow into the trees. Light seemed to be coming from deep within the forest, or was it her imagination? She hadn't noticed houses back there.

She went outside to look. Sleep was far from her reach at the moment. Too many life-changing thoughts spun around inside her head. Pine and the mossy bog scented the calm air. Silhouettes of tree branches appeared frozen against the twinkling star-filled sky. Scanning the forest, she no longer saw lights, nothing but the trees. It must have been a trick of the eyes. Walking along the edge of the meadow, she listened for night creatures. Nothing. How odd. In Maryland at night, she'd hear crickets, cicadas or frogs.

Then voices echoed across the open fields next to the castle.

Between the castle and the cottages, a half dozen cloaked figures headed right for her. They looked like monks or something out of a medieval horror story. Some of them carried lanterns. Druids? Hoods covered their faces. Dana stepped back into the shadows from the cottages and froze, blood pounding in her ears. As they passed, the hood of one of the cloaked figures slid back. It was Shannon. Another cloaked figure covered her again. Was that Damon? Then she heard women's voices, giggling and whispering. It was the entertainers from the show. All of them. Was Jack with them too?

They all rushed by, not seeing her hidden in the darkness. Entering the forest with only the light of a couple lanterns, they moved as if they had night vision goggles. How could they see where they were going with the dim lanterns? "Shannon? Shannon!" She called out to them but they didn't answer. She thought she heard someone call her name so, ignoring Mr. Donegal's and Jack's warning, she strode into the forest after them.

CHAPTER SIX

Mystical Forest

Dana followed the lamplights of the robed people who darted through the forest. When she could no longer see them, she used their voices as a guide. But the sounds shifted from far to her right one moment then far to the left. Was the darkness disorienting her? Her feet sank into soft, mucky earth, and smelled of damp, rotting leaves. She'd walked off the trail a dozen yards ago, but the lights from the cottages and the castle glimmered through the trees so she wasn't lost.

A shriek of laughter to her right sent her running in that direction again. Her feet stuck in mud. She turned and tried to back out but sank in deeper. The squishing sound from her feet blotted out the faint voices. Giving up on her pursuit, she tried backing out onto dry ground. Losing her balance, she slipped and fell into mucky water over her head. She struggled to the surface and screamed.

Spitting and sputtering the sour-tasting water, she swam to the muddy bank and tried climbing out, but slick, wet grass covered the bank and it was like trying to crawl up wet satin. Each attempt sent her slipping back into the water. Then strong hands gripped her wrists and dragged her onto dry ground.

When she got to her feet, she expected to see one of the robed people. "Let me go!"

"Dana, what're you doing out here?" Jack asked, still holding onto her. He didn't wear a robe, just jeans and a tee shirt.

"I fell in the bog. What does it look like? What are you doing out here?" She pulled free of him and planted her hands on her hips. Grass and muck hung from her arms, legs and clothes. She hated to think what was in her hair, what she smelled like.

"I heard you scream from my cottage. Come on. You need to get a hot shower, and I'll show you how to start a turf fire in your fireplace so you don't get pneumonia."

Standing on her cottage porch, Dana dug around her soggy sweatshirt pockets for her key. Not there. No key. But she felt something else. She pulled it out and stared at the brooch again. The one she'd placed in a drawer in her cottage. A chill went right down to her bones. "Holy crap."

"What's wrong?" Jack asked.

He'd think she was crazy. She stuffed the brooch in her jeans pocket. "I lost my key in the bog."

Jack started to laugh. "You didn't leave it in your room?"

"No, I didn't leave it in my room," she snapped. "It was in my sweatshirt pocket. Now what do I do? Can I get a spare at the office?"

"Sure." Jack laughed. "Tomorrow. The office is closed. Donegal's gone home for the night." He continued to laugh.

"It's not funny. Can't you break in or something?"

"Nope. Donegal would have my head. And I'd be paying for any damages."

Dana sighed and leaned against her door, defeated. "Terrific." The brooch was probably a joke, maybe an initiation for new members and she couldn't be bothered right now. But how did it get in her pocket?

"Dana, stay with me. I'll get you a key in the morning."

She thought for a moment, trying to figure out her options. She didn't have any. "I could check with one of the other girls in the troupe..."

"They won't be back for hours."

She gasped. "They were the ones in the robes? Are all the entertainers involved in whatever is going on in the woods? Are they doing some kind of pagan ritual?"

Jack pressed his lips together. "I'll explain it to you when the time is right but now you need yourself a shower to warm up. I'll give you something dry to wear."

She hesitated again. What choice did she have? She'd left the keys to her rental car and her purse with her money in her cottage. She couldn't even consider finding a place in town for the night.

"I'm being blunt here," Jack added. "Y'are shivering and smelling like a swamp. You'll be safe in my place. That be a promise."

"Okay," she said through chattering teeth.

As Jack led her into his cottage, she trembled more from the cold seeping into her bones than worry about spending the night in the one-room cottage. They'd been chatting by email for months so they were friends. Why shouldn't she trust him? The heat and attraction between them since she'd arrived couldn't be denied. She wondered if Jack felt it too.

Jack gave her towels, then a sweatshirt and sweatpants to wear. She took the brooch out of the wet jeans and stuffed it in the pocket of the sweat pants. If the piece of jewelry was valuable, she wanted to keep it safe. Tomorrow she'd take it to Mr. Donegal and find out about it. If it was an initiation or a joke, she wasn't about to tell Jack about it for some silly prank.

"I don't have a washer but I'll dunk your clothes in the sink with soap to get the bog smell out."

"Thanks." Dana's feet and hands were numb.

"Get yourself a hot shower now. I'll put the kettle on for tea and start a fire."

Much later, Dana sat on the floor in front of the fireplace, mug of hot tea in hand while Jack soaked her clothes including her panties and bra. Once finished with his task, he brought over a blanket and covered her shoulders, then sat beside her, rubbing her arms. "Y'are still shivering." The heat of the fire and Jack's touch penetrated her body and was making her horny. Without her underwear, her body felt ultra-sensitive beneath Jack's baggy clothes.

"A little, but I feel much warmer. What kind of wood are you burning in the fireplace? It has a sweet scent."

"It's not wood, it's turf, organic material cut from the bogs."

She stared at the blazing briquette. "Why not use firewood?"

"Not many trees. Lots of turf."

"It smells good and it's warm." She pulled her wet hair away from her neck and shivered.

"Hang on." Jack got up, went into the bathroom and returned with a comb. "Turn your back to the fire." He sat cross-legged beside her and ran the comb gently through her hair, lifting sections as he did, allowing the heat from the fire to dry her hair.

"Feels nice," she said, closing her eyes.

"You'll feel warmer once it's dry." He used his fingers to hold her hair away from her neck. Sensations skittered over her skin, tightening her nipples. As he continued, her body relaxed. The pleasurable stroking of her hair, the gentle caresses along her neck made her pussy wet and achy. She trembled a little, feeling her body come alive beneath his touch. Her clit throbbed. She was so aroused, she had to control the urge to turn around and pounce on him.

"It's going to curl wildly without a hair dryer to smooth it out," she said. Now the fire was too warm. She let the blanket fall from around her, and as it did, his oversized sweatshirt bared one of her shoulders. Her breasts swelled against the soft fabric, her nipples clearly protruding and sensitive.

"I like it curled. Beautiful and soft. Smells like my shampoo now instead of the bog."

She play-punched his thigh, which pressed against her hip. He laughed. Even though her hair was nearly dry, his fingers still combed through the strands and brushed the nape of her neck. God, it felt so good. She didn't want him to stop. Leaning into him, she wished his hands would slide from her hair and neck and move inside the shirt to her breasts.

It took all the willpower she had not to grasp his hands and guide them to her breasts. The attraction spiraled out of control. She'd sensed the sexual teasing during their chats on line, nothing too obvious. He'd maintained a friendly professionalism, but she suspected there was more. How much longer could she resist him? Getting involved with him probably would be a bad idea since she didn't know him all that well, and she'd be leaving by the end of summer.

Her cousin knew him, went to college with him. What was she worried about? Why did she have to over think everything in her life? Couldn't she be impulsive, spontaneous and indulge in some fun for once? That was the point for her taking this job, to get a break from her boring security job. She placed her tea mug down and slowly spun around to face him. His hands dropped from her hair and rested on his knees.

CHAPTER SEVEN

Don't Tempt Me

T here was no mistaking the lust in his gray-blue eyes. His lips parted slightly, as if ready to kiss her, but he didn't. She wondered if she waited for her to make the first move. He was letting her lead. If she wanted him, she could have him. She only had to give him a little encouragement. The sense of sexual power rushed through her, making her tingly all over. She slid the tip of her tongue over her lips, but still he didn't respond to her obvious hint. Her body was on fire now, and ached for him. Could she have misread his desire?

A muscle twitched at his jaw, a slight smile formed at his lips. "How are you feeling?"

"Good." She rested both hands on his arms. "And thanks for rescuing me and giving me a place to hang for the night."

"My pleasure." His voice sounded hoarse. He breathed deeply as his gaze dropped to her mouth then her breasts. Obviously, he wanted her. Why wouldn't he try to kiss her? Her awareness had awakened every nerve in her body, thinking about how his muscular body would feel against her damp skin.

The heat from the fire only added to her lust. She couldn't stop herself from what she did next. Her hands slid up his thighs, to his waist and moved along his sides. Jack let out a soft moan and shook his head.

What a fool she was. She had misinterpreted his desire. "I'm sorry, Jack. Guess I got a little carried away." She jerked her hands back and tried scooting away.

He let out a long breath. "I offered you a safe place to stay."

"I know." She watched him stare into the fire as if withdrawing from her. Shadows danced across his face and an awkward feeling twisted in her gut. Picking up one of those briquettes, he tossed it on the fire and jabbed it with a poker. Sparks shot up into the chimney. "Anything wrong?" she asked.

"You were frightened today by something. What was it?"

The question slammed into her as if he'd dunked her back into the bog. She swallowed. "I'm not sure if frightened is the right word. At first I was, maybe. Curious, confused, intrigued. I'm not sure how I feel."

He nodded. "Want to tell me about it?"

Studying his face, she saw concern and warmth in his eyes. "I don't know. I'm rather embarrassed by the situation, and I haven't been able to stop thinking about it. That's why I followed those people into the forest. I was curious too."

"What happened at the castle this afternoon?" He took her hand.

She felt as if she could trust him and it didn't seem like such a big deal now. "I went into the castle, even though Mr. Donegal said it was closed. I was enchanted by the place, wanted to look around, and find my harp. I saw a light flickering in the basement and thought there was a fire so I went to check it out."

"You found the dungeon." His mouth twitched into a slight smile.

"Two people were having a...sex."

"Really?" He held her gaze as if studying her response to the event. "Is that what scared you?"

"No, I mean, at first I thought the woman was in trouble because she was naked and tied up, hanging by her hands and feet. But then she seemed to be enjoying it quite a bit. And a man in a robe was whipping her." Dana shivered.

"Guess you've never done anything like that."

"No!" With Dana's abrupt answer, Jack glanced into the fire again.

"When you realized the woman was having a grand time, you took off?" He met her gaze so intensely, her heart leapt in her chest.

"No."

"No?"

"I couldn't stop watching. The woman was obviously in ecstasy. I don't think I've ever experienced that. And I thought I'd had a couple decent lovers in my past."

He chuckled. "Damon did say he thought you were getting turned on by watching."

"Damon told you I was there?"

"Yep."

"And you let me go through all the gory details?" Her face flushed, her pussy tingled, from the memory and from sharing it with Jack.

"Yep."

"Why?"

"Why do you think?" He grasped her arms and pulled her closer.

"You wanted to hear a good sex story?" She grinned.

Smiling, he shook his head. The smoldering look he gave her sent her heart fluttering. "I wanted to know about you. How you felt about that situation."

"Why?" But she had a feeling she knew the answer.

"To see how familiar you are with that lifestyle."

"Not very, I'm afraid. You?"

Jack regarded her with a heated gaze. The heat traveled from his hands to where he held her arms. She hoped he didn't let her go, and she had to hold her breath. "I'm a Dom. I've been in the lifestyle for years."

"Oh." Breathing again. His admission frightened her a little but she was more excited by it. "That's interesting. I'd like to hear more."

Had he been wondering about her during their flirty conversations online? Could he be fantasizing about torturing her the same way? She knew of this lifestyle from an erotic novel she'd read. Now that she thought about it, the story had shocked her then but also turned her on. She had been too embarrassed to talk about it with the boyfriend she'd been with at the time, but those fantasies had drifted into her mind during their lovemaking.

"Good answer," Jack said. Before she could say another word, he slipped his hand around to the back of her neck and lowered his warm lips to hers.

The slow, gentle kiss teased her mouth then he moved to her ear. Her fingers dug into his hips, wanting more, so much more. Every muscle melted in that kiss and she wanted it to go on forever. He released her, stroked her cheek with his fingers and already she ached to be kissed again.

She wanted to ask if all the entertainers in the musical troupe were into this lifestyle. And what was going on with those in the robes mysteriously disappearing in the forest? Was Jack involved in that too? But after that kiss, nothing seemed important. Later, she'd ask him later. Turning her head, she drew his mouth into a kiss again.

He moaned and parted her lips with his tongue. The intensity and heat surged through her body in sensuous waves. Hooking his arm under her knees, he pulled her across his lap and deepened the kiss. They both gasped for air.

Jack's clothes hung loose on her, and it wouldn't take much for her to wriggle out of them. The thought heightened her arousal, making her clit throb. She could feel the hard ridge of his engorged cock pressing against her thigh.

Skin, she wanted bare skin against her. She wanted him. Boldly, her hands slid under his shirt, across his hard abdomen to his chest and felt his arms tighten around her.

He grasped her breasts through the sweatshirt, then yanked it off, tossing it aside. His mouth captured one nipple and sucked it, rubbing the tip with his tongue. Fluttery sensations darted through her stomach.

Images of the extreme sex scene in the dungeon played over and over in Dana's mind. This was a side to her sensuality she must explore. Wrapping her arms around his neck, she met Jack's gaze. "Teach me. I want to understand what this is all about."

He closed his eyes and took in a breath, then looked at her for a long moment. "It's not for everyone."

"That's what I'd like to find out."

Abruptly, he pushed away from her, stood and walked into the kitchen area. She stared at the fire for a moment, deciding whether or not to press him. She put his sweatshirt back on. Finally, she got to her feet and went into the kitchen. "I struck a nerve. Can you tell me why?"

He nodded. "A woman I was involved with was curious about the D/s lifestyle. When she realized it wasn't for her, she left. It was hard on both of us."

"Well, you know ahead of time this would be a brief arrangement. I'm only here until the end of summer. Haven't you had a casual affair before?"

"A few at the clubs."

"Then we both know what to expect."

"Perhaps." But he didn't sound convinced.

"What's wrong with a summer romance and sexual exploration between two adults? I'll leave Ireland with fond memories of our hot liaison, and you might remember me as your sexy American fling." They would remain friends after. Wouldn't they?

He smiled a little. "I suppose that's one way to look at it."

Then a jolt of excitement mixed with fear struck her. Would he tie her up like Shannon? Part of her wanted to try that, and part of her was terrified of the idea. "Are you going to take me to the dungeon?"

"No."

Her insides wanted to scream at him in disappointment even though she didn't know if she was ready for that. "Why not?"

He let out a long breath. "Because I'm not sure it would be a good idea. But if I agree, there are things we should discuss first. Limits for one. I wouldn't want to do anything to make you feel uncomfortable working here. We need a harpist more than I need a submissive."

"Then we can take it step by step. I promise to let you know if something makes me feel uncomfortable." To Dana that seemed reasonable. "And I need this job, so I'm here for the summer."

Jack nodded and stepped closer. Cupping her chin with his hand, he gazed deeply into her eyes. Dana held her breath. "In the middle of a scene, you may not know what you can and can't handle. I need to know you well enough to recognize a situation that's become too intense for you, and anticipate your needs. I don't want to hurt you."

If ripping off her clothes would prove her desire for him, she'd do it. But throwing herself at him wasn't going to convince him of her hunger for exploring the kinky side of herself. "I don't know, Jack. I may not like a D/s lifestyle, or if I want to be your slave. I won't know unless I get a chance to try it out. I'm not afraid to find out if this kink is my kink. If you were an asshole, you'd be dragging me to the dungeon and hanging me upside down right now."

He smiled. "Don't tempt me."

"I'm serious. You're concerned about your partner's needs. That's good. How would we start?"

"There is a difference between a sub and a slave, but I won't go into that now," he added. "We'll begin by you calling me Master."

Her stomach did a twirl and her nipples puckered. "Yes, Master."

"Good." The hoarseness in his voice sent a jolt straight to her pussy. God, she wanted this badly, but didn't know exactly what she was getting into. Dana had to know if she was capable of experiencing pleasure through pain, submitting like she'd read in that BDSM book.

"The music I play on my harp may be sweet and delicate. That's not who I am."

He stared at her with a serious intent that made her breath catch. He was so handsome. His powerful shoulders and chest muscles tensed in the firelight. "Not too many women would chase after robed figures into a forest at night. Pretty ballsy."

"I saw Shannon and figured the others were the entertainers. I was curious."

He rubbed his forehead and sat down at the table. Was this his way of saying no? "Trust me, I'll tell you when a scene is too intense," Dana said. "We only have the summer to explore this. Why waste time?"

He shot her a dark look. "And what happens after the summer?" His words had a sharp edge.

She wanted to kick herself for that. "I have to go back to my old job by September first. Otherwise, I'll lose it. Do you want to spend the rest of your life wondering about what if?" She hesitated when he didn't answer and walked over and plopped down on the bed.

Jack came out of the kitchen, carrying a ladder-back chair. He placed it in front of the fire. "Stand up," he commanded. "Your first lesson begins now."

CHAPTER EIGHT

Sweet Submissive

Jack wasn't sure if he wanted to handle a summer fling. His gut told him it was a bad idea, having had more than his share of brief relationships in his younger days that had ended in disaster. The last one with Cleona had ripped at his gut. She was a natural submissive. She'd been vulnerable and unpredictable, and he'd taken his time. Just when he'd thought he'd reached her, gained her trust, awakened the deep desires he knew she suppressed, she'd decided to leave. Guilt and devotion to another man who wasn't hers, longing for another life, sent her away. This was not her world. She couldn't adjust and had returned to her own.

For months as Jack and Dana chatted online, he'd fantasized about her as his sub in a D/s scene. And here she was offering to be a willing participant. The eagerness in her beautiful brown eyes and the way her fingers stroked his arms and chest teased him and created thoughts of extremely distracting deeds.

Given a chance, he knew what pleasures he could offer her, what erotic fantasies he could fulfill. He stepped closer and lifted her chin with his fingers, holding her prisoner with his gaze. "If we do this, I'm willing to mentor you for a short time. As long as you understand I have no intentions of taking this any further. If you expect more, you'll be setting yourself up for heartbreak."

She nodded. "I can accept that, if you can."

He stepped back. Seeing her this close and eager was potent. How could he possibly refuse? "I can." He removed his shirt and tossed it onto the bed.

"Are you going to tie me up?" Dana asked as she stood. Crossing her arms over her waist, she pulled the sweatshirt over her head and tossed it on the bed next to his shirt. The firelight made her smooth skin glow and he noticed her nipples were hard. Her generous breasts hung in a slight teardrop shape. Not perfect, but beautiful to him. Jack's cock grew hard.

"For now, no. Stand in front of the chair and place your forearms on the seat. You may grasp the back if you like." She did as instructed. Her smooth, round ass showed nicely, even through the sweatpants.

"Like this?" she asked as she bent over and did as instructed.

"That's fine. Keep your legs straight but spread them." Immediately, she complied. "Good. You're comfortable? Warm enough?"

She nodded.

"Respond to my questions with, 'Yes or no, Master'. There's no right or wrong way to do BDSM. Whatever is satisfying, meets the needs of the couple and is consensual." He walked slowly around the chair, getting her used to his presence, and stroked her shoulder, nothing sexual yet.

"Yes, Master."

"A submissive may surrender to her Master but she controls the scene. If something becomes too intense for you, say the word 'slow', and I'll stop or slow down with what I'm doing." This time he slid his hand over her buttocks to register her response. She gasped and wriggled her ass. "If you want to end the scene completely say, 'red'."

"Okay. I understand."

"Dana, I always practice safe sex. And trust me never to hurt you." Moving his hands over her back, he slid them around to her breasts and she moaned. Like a content cat, she arched her back and closed her eyes. "Working with a virgin has its own unique charms."

She giggled. "I'm not a virgin, Master."

"To this lifestyle you are. And I did not ask you a question." He swatted her on her ass and she jumped, but didn't protest.

He went to his closet and brought out a small duffel containing a few implements: a rope, if he decided to tether her, and a suede flogger. The other items he left in the bag. She wasn't ready for them yet.

Was he making a mistake testing her this way? Moving too quickly? He didn't want to make her uncomfortable. First Damon and Shannon in the dungeon, then the group disappearing into the forest in robes and now him. What if she freaked out and decided to pack up and leave Ireland? The troupe would hang him. They didn't have the time to hire and train a new harpist especially with their busy season coming up.

It would be a lousy thing to do considering the troupe had helped him out by letting him stay in the cottage so he could save money to buy his uncle's place.

Playing sexual games with a curious novice could be setting himself up for disaster. Turning back toward the closet, he put the flogger, straps and ropes back. Then he sat onto the bed. "Dana, you can get up. This wasn't a good idea. It's late. You can sleep on the bed. I'll take the sofa."

"But I didn't say slow or red. Why did you decide not to…?"

He rubbed his forehead with his hand. The idea of mentoring her as a Dom aroused him. He hoped she didn't notice how hard his cock was. "Because we've only just met today." He grabbed a throw blanket and attempted to lie down on the sofa, which was a loveseat. No matter what position he tried, he couldn't get his large body to find a comfortable spot.

"Jack, we've been chatting for months online. Don't tell me you had no idea there was flirting going on between us." She grabbed the sweatshirt and pulled it back on again.

His mouth twisted in a half grin. "Yeah, you're right. We did have a few personal conversations."

"A few? One night you asked me what was my most sexually adventurous encounter."

"No way. I didn't ask... Oh yeah, I guess I did," Jack said dryly.

"You were fishing, trying to find out if I had been involved in a D/s relationship before." Dana stood and placed her hands on her hips, frowning. "If that wasn't flirting, what would you call it?"

"It's best we get some sleep now. We have a long day tomorrow." His sweatpants hung low on her hipbones and threatened to slide off. And he knew she wasn't wearing any underwear. Oh brother. He stared up at the ceiling.

"Look at you. You can't sleep on that. I'll sleep there. You sleep in the bed," Dana said.

He rose. "No. I'll take the floor."

"And freeze your ass off." She took a breath and lowered her voice. "Jack, we're not a couple of teenagers. I thought we were friends. We don't have to have sex just because we're in the same bed."

But God he wanted to. The bed did look more inviting than the floor. He'd behave though. He craved to hold her through the night, nuzzle his cheek against her breasts, curve his body against her round bottom, listen to her breathing while she slept. But to do so would be torture.

To feel her close throughout the night without fucking her would drive him mad. If he had a D/s scene with her, he might be able to relax and get some sleep. But that wasn't happening tonight. He doubted he'd be getting much sleep.

He'd turned his back toward the bed, so he couldn't watch her but she hadn't crawled into bed yet. She walked across the room and at first he thought she was stirring the fire. Instead she came out of the closet with the duffel and removed the flogger, straps, a rope and wrist restraints.

She laid them out across the bed then walked over to him and knelt in front of the loveseat and bowed her head. "Please, Master. Show me. I want to learn. I want to understand why I was scared by watching Shannon and

Damon and at the same time so turned on. I can't bear the thought of leaving Ireland at the end of summer without understanding these feelings. Every time I think of them, I get horny."

Her words triggered something deep within him. He couldn't deny the knot twisting in his chest, or the tug in his cock. Her reckless innocence thrilled him and he craved to claim her.

Oh hell. She was a sub and didn't even know yet. He'd have to take extra care with this one. It scared the hell out of him. What if she realized this wasn't her scene and panicked in the middle of a session? He didn't want to screw this up. He'd never been with a sub who was so green.

She let out a huff, spun on her heels and marched over to the bed. She picked up the leather cuffs and started strapping them around her wrists. "Dana, don't."

She gave him a pained look and continued to fasten the cuffs. Struggling with the wrist restraints, she managed to secure them to her wrists with the short length of chain dangling between the cuffs. Picking up the flogger, she walked over to Jack and knelt before him again, head bowed, and raised the flogger to him. "Please, Sir, I need to know."

His breath caught as he gazed at her naked from the waist up. Even his baggy sweatpants looked hot and sleazy. Far from the exotic fetish wear and lingerie he would see women in at Dagda's Edge, but so sexy. He stood and took the flogger from her. "You need to know what, slave?" It took a conscious effort to keep his voice firm and in control.

She let out a long breath. "I need to know if pain gives me pleasure."

He closed his eyes and took a breath. Fuck. She's definitely a sub. His cock twitched in response and rose to attention. Every ounce of resistance drained from his body. He'd have her, claim her and, the alpha male in him would lead her to explore her boundaries of both pleasure and pain. But it would be at his pace, and he'd walk away the first moment he realized this wasn't for her. Then the end of summer would arrive. What then? She'd leave him, return to her world in the US, like Cleona had returned to her home. At least he knew this now. He'd guard his heart and enjoy the pleasure. Willing himself to remain in control, he pointed to the chair. "Get into your original position."

"Yes, Master." She moved over to the chair, legs spread and bent forward at the waist with her hands gripping the chair back.

Heart racing, he had to remind himself, even if she was receptive, she wasn't a seasoned sub. "Remember your safe words?"

She nodded.

"Answer me, slave."

"Yes, Master. I remember the words." His hands stroked her buttocks, her back and moved around to cup her breasts. Then down each leg and up, barely grazing her pussy. She shivered a little and didn't resist. He hadn't removed the sweatpants yet. It wouldn't take much to slide them down. Once he felt the muscles in her back and shoulders relax, he picked up the rope and tied her arms and wrists to the chair.

He checked to make sure it wasn't too tight then picked up the flogger. She looked expectantly at him. "Eyes downcast, slave."

"Yes, Master." He took a number of practice swings and hit the bed, watching Dana jerk at the sound. Then he let the tassels hit her back in light strokes. She arched and moaned. As he moved over to her buttocks, he increased the power of his hits. She let out a couple of yelps but she didn't seem to have a problem handling the sensation.

"Painful, slave?"

"Not much, Master. More, please."

"Very well." He yanked down the sweatpants without giving her warning, drawing them to her ankles. She gasped but didn't struggle or protest. The flogger swung in circles again and swatted her butt cheeks on one side, then the other. He alternated the hits in a steady rhythm until her moans became shrill, then he brought her back down. He smoothed her reddened cheeks with his hands.

She panted now and wriggled her ass as he touched her. No whimpers of suffering, only moans of pleasure. He raised her chin, but she kept her eyes downcast as he requested. Such a good sub. How quickly she responded to his tasks and his touch. But he needed to study her expression and make sure she wasn't forcing her submission to please him. Her mouth opened with a lovely sigh, and she breathed normally.

"Are you with me, slave? Look at me."

She locked eyes with him. "Yes, Master. I'm fine. I'm with you. More, please."

He had to smile at that. "Are you wet?"

"Yes, Master."

"How wet?" His hand parted her labia and he slipped a finger inside her channel. Withdrawing his finger slick with her juices, he circled her clit and felt it harden and swell. "Very wet and aroused. More?"

"Yes." She gasped for a breath.

"Yes, what?"

"Yes, Master?"

"Good. Legs spread wide." Her ass twitched so nicely for him and when she opened her legs wider, he got a good view of her pussy. Swinging the flogger like a pendulum, he brought it up between her legs hard enough to make her body jerk. But his lovely slave didn't protest or move away. Her breathing deepened and sped up as he struck her pussy harder.

Moaning, she flinched with each strike.

"You could come like this?" he asked.

"Yes, Master."

"Hold back, don't come until I say. Understand? I must give you permission to climax. Your pleasure is within my control."

"I understand," she said through gritted teeth. "God, it's so good."

"Tell me when you're close."

"Now. I'll come if you continue like this, Master."

He stopped stimulating her with the flogger and rubbed her ass and back. "You did well, slave."

"Will you make me come now?" Her voice was shaky, practically begging.

"No. This is the end of your first lesson. It's time for you to rest."

"But..."

"Your pleasure will exceed your fantasies if you can surrender to me." He untied her, brought her to the bed and cradled her in his arms. As much as his body wanted more of her, to make love, he'd wait. Control and trust made a brittle foundation in a new D/s relationship, especially when the sub was inexperienced. He knew he'd left her aching for release and that was good. Once she learned he controlled her pleasure, trusted him enough to surrender all sensations, her release would be more intense than she could imagine. Best not to overwhelm his sweet slave just yet. Besides, he'd promised her a safe place to stay the night.

CHAPTER NINE

Black Robe

The next morning, Dana woke to the smell of bacon simmering in a frying pan and brewing coffee. Stretching under the warmth of the covers, she gazed at Jack as he prepared breakfast. Shirtless, barefooted, with jeans hung low on his hips. His hair looked as if he'd tried to smooth it down with his fingers, but sections stuck out, still mussed from sleep.

God, he looked hot. The sight of him made her horny all over again, especially since she'd gotten no release. At least he'd satisfied a little of her curiosity about the D/s lifestyle. For the moment, she'd trust that his plan for slow steps into his world was the best. She hoped he wouldn't take too long.

The chair she'd been tethered to stood in front of the cold fireplace. Memories of their bizarre night seemed like a dream now except for her tender bottom. The thought sent a rush of warmth straight to her pussy and her clit throbbed. Yes, pain did give her pleasure. The whole experience was strangely exciting but also unsettling.

She didn't know how she felt about the need to be dominated. Was this something she could do in a relationship all the time? Or was she trying something new, just to say she did it? Like parachuting. A thrill-seeking thing. Once she'd done it a few times, she could say she'd had the experience but it wasn't something she'd care to do regularly.

This type of lifestyle required trust. But how could she trust Jack if she didn't know if she could trust herself? She'd taken a break from her well-paying job to be a musician in Europe. A responsible thirty-something didn't do that. That was what her parents told her anyway. "Morning," she called out to Jack. "Smells wonderful."

He turned around. "Morning. Sleep well?"

She got up, not shy about being naked, and enjoyed the up-and-down look he gave her. "Slept good, considering." She smiled as she rubbed her bottom with her hand.

"Sore?"

"A little, but in a good way." She found his discarded sweatshirt and pants and slipped them back on.

"You seemed to enjoy it. Did you feel I pushed too far?" He speared the browned bacon slices in the pan and drained them onto a paper towel, then poured off the grease into the sink.

"No, I was fine. I'm ready for the next lesson."

He stirred beaten eggs into the hot pan with a spatula. "Good." His voice became husky. "After the show tonight meet me in the dungeon."

Her stomach clenched. "Where I saw Damon and Shannon?"

"Yes. Wait for me there immediately after the show. And I want to find you completely naked when I arrive. Understand?"

"Yes, Master."

After they finished eating, Dana helped clean up and straighten the bed.

"Your clothes haven't dried completely and they still smell like the bog," Jack said. "I'll take a run up to the office and get another key for your cottage. You can wait here."

Dana looked down at Jack's clothes. "Thanks. It would be a little obvious walking around in your sweats."

"Be right back." He pulled her into his arms, gave her a kiss, then released her. "Looking forward to tonight."

"Me too."

When the door closed, Dana folded a throw blanket and placed it on the end of the bed. She picked up the flogger, wrist straps and ropes and opened the closet to put them away.

A long, black robe hung in the closet, like the one she saw the other entertainers wearing last night. She gasped and stepped away from the closet and shoved the door closed.

Jack was part of this secret group too. What was this all about? What would've happened if she hadn't fallen into the bog? What if she'd caught up to them and stumbled into whatever they were doing?

Images of bizarre sacrifices or rituals came to mind. She'd seen one too many creepy movies. Walking to the back of the cottage, she peeked between the curtains out the window, trying to see into the forest. She couldn't see anything through trees and shrub growth. The sky was clear and the paths into the woods could easily be seen. She wouldn't fall into the bog in the daylight.

She didn't know much about pagan practices but had a friend who was Wiccan. If the entertainers were a pagan group, she had nothing to worry about. A black robe didn't mean they practiced black magic. She laughed at herself but it was a forced laugh.

The door to the cabin swung open and Dana jumped. "It took some persuading, but Donegal finally gave me the key. He couldn't believe you went into the forest at night after he warned you."

"What did you tell him?" She hadn't gotten the nerve to ask him about the robe yet. He was grinning and his eyes sparkled with mischief but not evil. There couldn't be anything evil about him, could there?

"Mr. Donegal is very superstitious. I'm afraid I told him you saw someone walk into the woods and you thought it was Shannon. You followed her. I wasn't lying. He assumed you saw a ghost. He asked me to keep an eye on you and protect you from anything supernatural. 'The forest is haunted,' Donegal says."

"Haunted?"

"No, it's not. I've lived here all my life. Never seen a ghost." Jack handed her the key. "He told me to tell you to stay out of the forest."

"Thanks for the key. See you later." She rushed past him, suddenly wanting to get far away from that black robe.

"You okay? Aren't I taking you to town?"

"Oh, right."

He gave her a puzzled look. "Go and get changed. I have a surprise for you."

CHAPTER TEN

Leather and Longing

J ack gave Dana a tour of the old town and pointed out grocery stores, pubs, restaurants and other shops. She couldn't wait to go exploring and browse through the quaint shops. Before their stop at the grocery store, he brought her to an older part of town where the streets narrowed and flower boxes or hanging baskets decorated store windows. The smell of baked bread and smoked meat wafted in the air. "I'm getting hungry again," Dana said. "Something smells good."

"This is where I got the brown bread for your dinner." He pointed to a bakery. "Next door is a good place for meats. My uncle's place is around the corner. I'm trying to get a loan to buy it."

"Your uncle can't hold a loan for you?"

"It would be a hardship for him. He wants to retire. And the place needs some work." Jack opened the door to a shop with a sign that read "Keagan's Wool Shop"

The store was quite spacious inside with several racks of woolen sweaters, coats and wraps. Wooden shelves lined the walls filled with neatly folded colorful knits. "Look at all the beautiful things." Dana strolled around the room, touching the soft knits. "I always thought wool sweaters would be scratchy. These are so soft."

He pulled out a gray tweed wrap and covered her shoulders with it. "Like it?"

"It's gorgeous. It's like a gray cloud with bits of purple in it. I'm sure I'll be back to shop here."

"My uncle will love to see you. This one's a gift."

She was about to argue with him, when a gentleman came out from a back room. "I heard that. I'll be taking that out of your paycheck," the man said with a wink. He smiled at Dana and had the same mischievous sparkle in his eyes as Jack only this man was about seventy years old.

"Uncle Lee, this is Dana. She's from America and our new harpist."

Dana held out her hand and shook Lee's. "Nice to meet you. I love your shop."

"America? A long way to come for a job," Lee said. His voice held a note of disapproval.

"My cousin lives in Dublin and she heard about the job. She and Jack went to college together. I'm here just for the summer."

"Ah, so you're a student?"

"No, I took a temporary leave from my management job in a security company. I'll be returning to my position at the end of summer."

Lee's face scrunched up. "A manager? You left a good job? Aren't you a little old to be acting like a rebellious teenager?" His voice was tight. Dana didn't know what to say.

"Uncle," Jack cut in. "Maybe she had a good reason to leave."

"When you're young, you can be reckless and have a traveler life, drifting from place to place, job to job like a gypsy. When you're an adult, you stick with a job even if you don't like it. That's how you stay off the streets."

Jack was about to argue but Dana jumped in.

"No, your uncle has a point. If I had a family, I probably would've made a different choice, but sometimes taking a risk opens up opportunities. I don't want to look back on my life and wonder what if, or if only I had…" She glanced at Jack then at Lee. She obviously wasn't scoring any points with his uncle. "I might be making a mistake, but we learn from mistakes and become stronger from them." She should shut up before she dug herself in deeper.

"It's foolish." Lee's face was red. He headed into the other room then glanced back at Jack. "Look around if you like. I have the kettle on if you'd like some tea. Got a letter today. You were turned down on that last loan."

Jack swore under his breath. "Did they give a reason?" He held up his hand. "Forget it, I don't want to know. They're all stupid reasons. Out-of-town banks say the tourist trade has dropped off and a shop in this area is too much of a risk. Local banks say they remember my wild, reckless days in college and don't think I'm a responsible businessman. That was thirteen years ago. Other reasons mention the leather and specialty items are not appropriate merchandise. Certain months of the year we make more on those items than the woolen goods." Jack shook his head. "I've sold everything I own, given up my apartment to buy this place and it looks like it's not going to work out."

Lee frowned. "If I took out part of the loan."

"No. You've been trying to retire for seven years. You've worked hard all your life. I'm not going to have you sacrifice because of me. You could get a buyer for this place and live comfortably. If I can't buy it in three months, then it goes on the market and I find another job."

"Don't worry about it, Jack. There's time." Lee glanced over at Dana and gave her a nod. "I'll get the tea."

After Lee went into the other room, Dana turned to Jack. "I'm sorry if I upset your uncle."

Jack groaned. "You didn't. He doesn't understand. Things were different in his day." He took her hand. "Come on, I have something to show you."

"Is this the surprise?"

"Yeah."

Jack showed Dana into a room separate from the clothing section. It had a sign that said "Adults Only", which he pointed out to her. Opening the door, he led her through and kept an eye on her expression. He wanted to see her response when she viewed the various items and devices.

Upon scanning the room, Dana studied the display of leather fetish wear and extensive selection of bondage accessories and implements for a sadomasochist's dream. "Wow, this is amazing." She walked around and felt the leather floggers, held up a leather vest and frowned at the mask and ball gag. A few contraptions she examined for a long time. By the look in her eyes, she appeared more fascinated than shocked. He was relieved at that.

"What do you think?"

"It looks like an amusement park for the sadomasochist."

Jack laughed.

"I think I'd need an instruction manual on most of this stuff."

Jack agreed. "A lot of it does come with instructions and warnings." She didn't seem offended by anything in the room, but in the back of his mind he had his concerns. He picked up a flogger and swung it in the air and gave her a wicked grin.

"I like those, I discovered."

"I know." His smile faded. "Something my uncle said made me think. Why did you leave your job? Is coming to Ireland a rebellious diversion?"

She picked up a braided cat and ran her fingers through it. "The security business is a job I've had since high school. I went to college for electrical engineering and minored in music. My parents are supportive about me playing the harp but not as a career. I always dreamed of playing in a large symphony but it would never pay like my management job. My cousin knows I love Ireland and has been urging me to spend the summer with her for years. When she told me about the medieval show, I knew this was my last chance to follow a dream."

"So, you'll be going back," Jack said.

She let out a breath. "Yes, that's what I had planned."

"If you had the opportunity would you consider staying here?"

She didn't answer right away. "That would be a hard adjustment. I'd be so far away from my friends and family."

He nodded. "And what about this part of your life?" He held up some bondage straps. "Is this a lifestyle you're considering after last night or is this a rebellious phase like leaving your job?" He tried to keep his tone light but could hear an edge to his voice. He remembered how willing Cleona was at first to explore a D/s relationship, but it didn't last. Maybe their differences had as much to do with her decision to return to her vanilla sex life. It had taken a long time to get over her. Was he insane to consider getting involved with another novice? Dana's arrival had set off a rush of emotions he hadn't anticipated. If he had any sense, he'd avoid her.

"I think it's too early for me to make that decision, Jack."

"Fair enough." If she agreed, he'd set himself up for another fall, knowing at the end of summer, she would leave

She moved to him, her lips a breath away. "But I am getting wet and horny standing in this room, so that must count for something. Right?"

His cock hardened at her words. "It certainly does." He would probably hate himself by the end of summer but he couldn't resist a willing submissive as beautiful as Dana. "I'm convinced you're ready for the next step. The dungeon."

* * *

When Dana first got back to her cottage, she'd pulled out the brooch from Jack's sweatpants and placed it on the dresser. She made a quick list of grocery items, took a brief stop in her bathroom and stuffed some cash in her purse. Rehearsal wasn't until the afternoon so she had plenty of time to make a quick run to town to shop then practice until she had to meet with the troupe.

On her way, she'd drop off the brooch to Mr. Donegal. But the brooch was not sitting on the dresser where she'd left it. Swearing under her breath, she dropped to her hands and knees and began searching on the floor, under chairs and the bed. Nowhere. What the hell happened to it?

She gazed around the room, trying to think where she could've dropped it, or if she had moved it and had just forgotten.

Was she losing her mind? She was about to give up and leave the cottage when she noticed something glittering on the costume hanging on the closet door. The brooch was pinned above the left breast area of the dress. She knew she hadn't placed it there. Or had she? Was she so jet lagged that she couldn't remember?

Had someone sneaked into her room while she was in the bathroom to play a prank on her? Joke or not, she was creeped out. She grabbed her purse, took the brooch and headed to the gate house to speak with Mr. Donegal.

She walked up to the desk and Mr. Donegal glanced up over the top of wire-rimmed glasses. He'd been studying a file of papers. "Good morning, Mr. Donegal."

"Mornin'." Slowly he stood and approached the desk. "What can I do for you?"

"I want to turn in this brooch. I found it in my room." She held it out to him and felt a tug in her chest. It was a lovely piece and would've looked nice on her costume. But it wasn't hers to keep.

He took the pin and turned it over in his hand, but didn't say anything.

"I thought a previous guest might've left it in the cottage, or maybe it's an antique from the castle."

"We do rent those cottages out to tourists sometimes, but no one has stayed in that one for months. I'm sure the housekeeper would've found it. And it's not an antique from the castle." He handed it back to her. "Cheap souvenir, not worth much. You're welcome to keep it."

"Oh, okay. Thanks." Dana wasn't sure if she liked the idea or not. Was she being silly thinking the pin had strange powers? Jet lag and stress had invaded her common sense. The brooch would look lovely on her costume or the new wrap Jack got her, cheap trinket or not.

CHAPTER ELEVEN

Meeting Her Knight

"Let the banquet begin!" Jack announced to the crowd of guests seated in the main dining hall of the castle. With his words, medieval-clad servers brought out platters of soup and warm brown bread to each table for the first course while Dana and the other musicians performed a lively Renaissance melody and Jack and Shannon sang a duet. Their voices echoed beautifully around high stone walls.

When he'd said he was one of the singers, she had no idea how gifted he was. In her opinion he could be singing in a Broadway show. He looked so handsome in his period costume; the brocade tunic cinched with a leather belt fit nicely. The tights he wore, she remembered laughing at earlier. Jack's comment had been, "Something wrong, my lady?" The thought brought a smile to her, and she caught Jack winking at her now as if he knew she was thinking how hot he looked.

Or was he thinking about later, after the show? Earlier in his cottage, he'd instructed her not to wear panties under her costume. This, he said, was a simple test of her subservience and only they would know. After the show, he said he would meet her down in the dungeon for a more intense session.

Heat traveled through her body and her nipples tightened beneath the green brocade dress. The corset-like bodice pressed her breasts in rounded mounds above the lacy trim. Moving her arms while stroking the harp was restraining not to mention difficult for breathing.

Under the long skirt, Dana spread her legs and held her harp in the proper position between them. But without wearing panties, her chemise brushed over her bare pussy, making her more sensitive and wet each minute. And by the added movement of her playing, her clit swelled. She wanted Jack's hand between her legs, touching her slit, rubbing her. Every sensitive nerve throbbed as she plucked each note in the song.

Jack glanced her way, a slight smile on his lips. Could he tell she was turned on? Would he do the things to her that Damon did to Shannon? Heat traveled to her face and she could hardly focus on her performance.

Halfway through the dinner, Shannon sang a solo and Damon played the violin. No other musical pieces or singers participated. The other entertainers stood and moved to the side of the room.

Jack graciously took Dana's hand and led her offstage for the performance. While they were aside he whispered into Dana's ear. The movements he did in a theatrical way so that it appeared to the audience his conversation was part of the show. "You're naked beneath your dress?"

"Yes." Dana followed his lead for the sake of the audience. They were acting like two peasants carrying on a little mischief while the lead performers entertained the lord's guests in the castle. Although the guests could not hear the real conversation.

"After the show," Jack whispered in Dana's ear, "take that door down to the dungeon and close it behind you. There's a sign on it that says 'No Admittance, Staff Only'. When all the guests have left, I'll meet you there."

"Okay, I'll wait for you in the dungeon. It's safe?" Her pulse raced now because many of the guests were nearly finished with their dinner.

"Yes, it's very safe. No one will disturb us. The others have plans tonight. There's a turf fire already in the fireplace so you'll be warm enough."

"Warm enough for what?" Her voice was shaky and she felt a little afraid.

"A lounger is in front of the fire. Wait there. After you've removed your dress and all your—" Jack's brow creased. He touched her brooch. "Where did you get that?" She didn't appreciate the accusation that edged his sharp tone.

She couldn't exactly tell him it mysteriously appeared in her sweatshirt pocket. "Beautiful isn't it? I found it in my cottage. I tried turning it in to Mr. Donegal, but he told me to keep it."

His gaze narrowed. "Don't wear it again. It's not part of the costume."

"Really? It looks like an antique and the Celtic design is similar to a pendant I saw Shannon wearing."

"Shannon might know who it belongs to," he offered.

"Of course, I didn't think to ask her. It might belong to one of the members. I'll show it to her later." Dana placed her fingertips over the pin. She hated the idea of giving up her little souvenir.

"I'll give it to her. You'll be going to the dungeon right after the last song." He arched a brow.

Reluctantly, she removed the brooch and placed it in his hand. She hated giving it up, but if it didn't belong to her, she shouldn't keep it of course. "If she doesn't know whose it is, or if no one claims it, I'd like to have it."

He nodded. "It might belong to Jane, the woman who's on maternity leave." He patted her bottom, then gave it a squeeze.

She gasped, glancing shyly into the crowd. There was a snicker in the audience, and Dana covered her mouth. Leaning into Jack, she whispered, still trying to play a part and hide her anxiety. "You want me to be completely naked before you come down?"

"Yes. If you're not naked, then I'll know you're not ready for the dungeon scene."

"No, I want to do this."

"Good. Then, my lady, after the banquet, your dungeon awaits." He took her hand and led her back to her harp for the final performance of the show.

After the show, Dana waited for the guests and entertainers to leave the hall then walked down the spiral staircase in her medieval costume. She felt as if she'd stepped back in time for a moment, as if she was a maiden sneaking off to meet her knight.

When she entered the dungeon, she smelled the sweet woody scent of a turf fire blazing in the large fireplace. Even though the room was lit by sconces on the walls, centuries of soot darkened the stones. A straight-backed chair stood by the bottom of the stairs and a lounger sat in front of the fire. The lounger looked comfortable but the rest of the items scattered around the room looked like devices straight out of a Dark Ages torture chamber.

The hammock swing with all its chains and straps hung from eye hooks in the ceiling. Another slanted bench with various pads and straps stood next to the swing. A table contained numerous items like floggers, handcuffs, dildos, condoms, a pitcher of water and a few other things she couldn't identify. One of the black robes hung from a hook on the wall. Her body began to shake. Her pulse thrummed in her ears. This was going to happen.

With shaky hands, she unbuttoned her dress and let the bodice slip from her shoulders. The cool air whisked across her skin and her nipples instantly puckered.

Bare from the waist up, Dana approached the angled bench with the straps. She knelt on the pads and rested her forearms on the other side of a raised cushion. Ah, now she got it. This was used for either spanking or fucking from behind. Her chest tightened. Would Jack try fucking her ass? She wasn't fond of that. She could always use the safe word if she didn't like what he did.

Dana was so hot she didn't care where he fucked her—on this restraining bench, in the swing or on the lounger by the fire. All of it was a little frightening but she was more turned on than she'd ever been in any other relationship. Wet heat gathered between her legs.

In the shower this morning, she'd shaved herself smooth and her tender skin tingled. On the table she found a set of metal clamps with a chain. Nipple clamps. Shannon had worn these when she'd interrupted their encounter.

She cringed and couldn't imagine how that kind of pain could be pleasurable. They looked as though they would hurt. Picking them up, Dana tried to pinch them onto her hardened nipples. "Ouch!" she cried out and the clamps dropped onto the table. She tried again and got one clamped. The pain was sharp but after a moment she got used to it. She attempted the other, but it kept slipping off.

"You're not naked," Jack said from behind her.

Dana yelped and spun around, the nipple clamp dangling from one nipple. "Jack." He had his brocade costume draped over his arm and wore the white silk shirt and jeans. The shirt was open at the neck a few buttons. Damn, he looked good. "You changed."

"I guess you're not ready for the dungeon." His voice held a tone of disappointment. "Get dressed. Maybe another time." He turned and started back up the stairs.

CHAPTER TWELVE

Surrender to Me

"No, Jack, wait. I was distracted by all the devices. I was trying the nipple clamps. Without much success, I might add." She laughed, trying to lighten his dark mood. "I guess I need some instruction." She let the clamp hang from one nipple as she gazed into his eyes.

He came back into the room. "A submissive who doesn't follow her Master's orders is asking for punishment," he said firmly.

"Then I suppose I deserve to be punished," she said, her voice edged with defiance. The thought of punishment didn't frighten her at all even though her body trembled. She hoped he would use the flogger on her again to relieve the ache that inflamed her. "But what if someone had come down here before you did and I was naked?"

"What if they did? Some women like being watched."

An odd answer, she thought. "I don't."

He smiled. "You're safe here."

"Yes, you said." She relaxed a little, glancing around at the other contraptions in the room. "I'm still new at all this. How about you show me how this works? It looks like fun." She pointed to the slanted bench with the pads and straps.

Pressing his lips together, Jack tensed his jaw. He placed his costume on a straight-backed chair by the door. Then he moved closer to her, removed the nipple clamp and tossed the item on the table. Lifting her chin, he gave her a gentle kiss. "This isn't a game. It's true a sub or a slave has all the power, even the control of a scene. One word can slow or stop what's happening at any time." His lips were a breath away from hers. The warm, moist heat of his mouth and tongue drifted to her ear and down her neck.

"I understand that," she breathed, her eyes closed as she indulged in his touch. His hands skimmed over her breasts and the pads of his thumbs rubbed her already raw nipples, which made her clit throb. "Not a game," she echoed.

His hands moved lower and finished unbuttoning her dress and chemise and let them drop to the floor in a pile of green brocade while his fingers slid up her thighs and over her hipbones, gliding toward her pussy but not touching her sensitive flesh. God, she wanted him to pleasure her there. She resisted the urge to beg for it. He was the Master and she the sub.

"It's more like a dance when two people try to lead. You're tugging each other in different directions on the dance floor. When one person leads, and you both hear the beat of the music, the dance is like magic. Does that make sense to you?" He drew her close and she felt the warmth of his hard body through his shirt.

"Yes." One arm held her possessively against him as his other hand worked her pussy. "That feels good." Dana arched her back and wriggled her hips.

Then he slipped a finger deep into her cunt. She gasped as a jolt of intense pleasure shot through her. "You want more?"

"Yes, more, Master."

His thumb circled her clit and her knees buckled. If he kept moving his hand and finger in just that rhythm, she could come. She craved it. "That's incredible."

"Your clit is swollen and your pussy dripping. I bet I could make you come like this. Am I right?"

"Yes." She gripped his shoulders to keep from falling.

"Am I your Master?"

"Yes." She rocked on his hand, fucking his finger. When she moved just right, he'd hit her G-spot at the same time. "Please, Master, let me come."

To her disappointment, he withdrew his finger from her channel and slowed the stimulation of her clit. "Not without my permission, and not yet. As your Master, I control your pleasure. I'll tell you when you can come. When you do get close to an orgasm you tell me the word, edge. I'll know to slow down, or give you more, depending on my mood."

She nodded as the peak of her orgasm faded. Damn it, she'd been so close.

"We'll go at this slowly."

"I don't know if I can go slowly," Dana argued. "What if I were to come without your permission?"

"Your punishment would be more severe." He turned to the slanted bench. "You need a bit of punishment for not following my order before." He stroked her buttocks in a gentle caress. Was he trying to let her know he wasn't cruel with his gentle touch? His words were firm and they made her pulse kick up a few beats. She longed for the punishment almost as much as she ached for the release of an orgasm.

What was wrong with her? Was this normal?

"Yes, Master. I need to know." Her voice almost broke with emotion. She took a breath and tried to relax. But how could she if she was naked and he wasn't? His strong hands teased her bare pussy and got her so worked up she wanted to scream.

"Need to know what, slave?" A grin twitched at the corner of his mouth. His hand brushed her hair back so tenderly her throat tightened.

She swallowed. "To see if I can feel the intense passion that Shannon seemed to feel while she was in that swing."

He smiled. "I think you will. If you trust me, and surrender to me. But you'll need to communicate your needs during and after a scene. If I'm about to do something you're not sure about or you can't handle, use the safe words to slow or stop."

"I'll remember. 'Red' to stop. And 'slow' to slow things down."

"Tell me when you like what I'm doing too."

She glanced over toward the stairs leading to the great room but she didn't mention her hesitation.

"We won't be disturbed here."

She wasn't so sure but she wouldn't argue with him. She wanted him so badly she didn't care anymore if someone did come down those stairs. Heat swept over every inch of her body. She wanted him now. "Thank you, Master."

"Clasp your hands behind your back." She did and watched as Jack unbuttoned his shirt, yanked it off, then slid off his jeans and tossed them on the chair. The bottom dropped out of her stomach when she noticed his hard cock. The smooth pecs and rigid abdomen, the cut of muscles in his thighs and ass, made her ache to have him in her bed. Then he stroked her breasts in a gentle, sensuous manner, pinching the nipples between thumb and forefinger tighter and tighter until she yelped in pain. "You'll handle the clamps quite well."

She gasped as a shimmer of heat coursed through her body.

Although he'd told her to keep her hands behind her back, she wanted to roam them over his magnificent chest, down his stomach and take his thick cock in her hand. But she'd submit to him, learn the ways of a submissive because by doing so she might reach that state of ecstasy that Shannon had. More than that, she wanted to please him, wanted to give over the control.

Jack's mouth captured a nipple and tugged on it, and his teeth scraped across the tender skin. He worked the other nipple in the same way until they both were raw and puckered. "Feel good?"

"Yes, very."

He stepped over to the table and picked up the nipple clamps and approached her. "I'm going to clamp your nipples now." Dana bit her lower lip, anticipating the pain. As he tightened the clamp, the pain increased but she tried to work through it. The pain became excruciating but at the same time a jolt of pleasure shot to her pussy. She closed her eyes and moaned, part from the pain and part from the pleasure.

Then the pressure eased up a bit. "Brave girl," he said with a short laugh. "You're not telling me when you're feeling too much pain. But fortunately, you have very expressive eyes. Is that better?" He adjusted both clamps until there was pressure and a slight amount of discomfort but the kind that was pleasurable.

"Better, yes."

"Now kneel," he ordered.

She knelt on the slant bench, and Jack strapped her forearms and ankles down. Her upper body rested lower on a padded board so her ass was elevated.

His hand slid over her ass and around to her slit. "I've made you wet." His finger slid over her clit. "Yes, I think you're ready."

Her body quivered and she tugged against the restraints as a climax quickly approached. "You're going to make me come, Master." She hoped. If she didn't come soon or get fucked soon, she'd jump out of her skin.

"No, I'm going to punish you, remember?" He pulled his hand away. "And don't come yet. Not until your punishment is over."

"Yes, Master," she sighed.

Jack picked up a flogger from the table and caressed her with the leather lashes down her back and ass, making her shiver. "Relax. If you let go the pain can bring pleasure."

Her teeth clamped tight, anticipating the first hard blow. Jack moved around to the front of the bench and bent to kiss her. He used his tongue to part her lips and deepen the kiss. She moaned and relaxed. Then he stood, moved beside her and swatted her ass with the flogger. It hurt, a lot. She tensed and bit her lip, determined not to cry out. The tails of the flogger struck again and again, equally on each side until her skin burned. Briefly, he stopped and rubbed her ass.

"Hmmm. Turning a little pink now." His fingers followed the curve of her hip, slipping down the cleft of her ass and probed the opening of her anus with the tip of his finger. "How would you like it if I fucked you here?" He pressed a little harder but her sphincter muscle tightened. Her body jerked.

She didn't know what to say to him, she didn't want to call an end to their evening.

"I would love to take your ass like this but I can tell by the way you're tensing, you're not quite ready for that. We won't go there tonight. Another night then."

"Yes, Master." Her words sounded slurred to her.

The smacks of the flogger began again. She closed her eyes, floating with the pain, feeling her heart throb in her temples. As the pain increased, her skin tingled and her clit swelled. Juices from her pussy dripped down her thighs. She couldn't move. Trapped, but she had no desire to escape. The pounding in her head increased, not a headache, more like a head rush. Any moment she would scream, "Fuck me, Jack". It took all her willpower to keep from crying out.

He walked over to the table and dropped the flogger, picked up a condom and slipped it on.

Strapped down onto the bench, she felt helpless, completely under his control. A flutter of panic rose to the surface. But then Jack moved in front of her, claiming her lips again, and kissed her until she gasped for breath. Watching him step back, she felt the heat build inside her and desperately craved his touch. She admired the rigid thickness of his cock and had to feel that fullness deep inside her. His hands slid over her back, her breasts, easing the tension from her body. "Let's see how ready you are for me."

His hand moved over her bottom and between her legs, then he plunged a finger deep into her dripping cunt. "God, yes, Master." She arched her back, tugging on the restraints.

He buried his finger deep. Her body bucked. "You're ready for me to make love to you then?" His words were so tender, she could cry.

"Yes, please take me, Master. I want you." Every muscle in her body trembled with need. Jack knelt on the bench between her legs and nudged the head of his cock at her entrance. Easing in just enough to open her cunt, he then stopped. Her pussy clenched, aching for all of him. She whimpered. Sweet torture. Restrained as she was, Dana's pleasure was completely under his control. "Please, Master. Fuck me deep."

Grasping her hips, he eased in and out of her in small movements. Reaching around her hip, he pressed his fingertips onto her engorged clit. The pressure was almost too much to bear but it felt so good. Then he thrust hard into her all the way to the hilt of his shaft.

Dana cried out. Her head spun. The restraints inhibited her ability to move, heightening her pleasure. The pressure and slight movements on her clit and the rhythmic thrusts of his cock sent her racing toward an orgasm. "Master, I'm going to come soon." She felt the tension building in her sex. If he told her not to, she wasn't sure how she could stop.

"Come for me, come for me now." It was an order not a request, and the command in his voice sent her over the edge.

She screamed as the waves of her climax radiated through her, the intensity more powerful than any orgasm she could remember. "God, yes."

When he let out a low groan, he grasped her hips, and she felt his cock pulsing inside her. He wrapped his arms around her body, holding her captive with the restraints still bound to her. Quite some time later, he slipped his cock from her body and leaned back. Gently, he stroked her body, shoulders, breasts and ass. His hands moved in slow, sensuous touches. Her mind and body drifted as if she was floating on a raft in the ocean.

She glanced at the black robe hanging on the wall and thought of the entertainers in the forest. What were they doing in there? Was Jack a part of it? Could they be drawing her into some bizarre, evil thing? Or had she watched too many horror movies?

"You're so beautiful." She heard Jack speak, but he sounded far away now.

Someone touched her between her legs and it felt good. Jack? Of course, it was Jack. Were there more than two hands? Or was it her imagination? Shadows danced around the room from the flickering flames. She imagined other people touching and stroking her, bringing her closer to another climax. Almost there.

Then she heard voices, men mostly as they cried out in pain. The crack of a whip pierced the air which had turned stifling and smelled of sweat and other unpleasant human odors. A man cried out in searing pain. Not the pain and pleasure of a BDSM scene. This sound was of a man being tortured. Cold seeped into her blood and she shivered. Was she dreaming or hallucinating?

Her gaze fell upon the black robe again, and she wanted to get away from it. The voices and smells didn't go away. Dana tried to lift her arms, her legs. She couldn't.

Trapped. Panic gripped her. She struggled against her restraints. She had to get out, get away from them.

Far away, she heard Jack's voice, but she wasn't sure what he said. Dana drew in a breath. Her panic and fear sucked the air out of the room. She had to get out, now!

Then she remembered.

"Red!"

Like a fire alarm, when Jack heard Dana's safe word, he instantly yanked off the Velcro straps two at a time, both wrists, then ankles and lifted her off the bench. Searching around the room, he looked for a blanket, then cursed himself for forgetting that one item when he'd set up this scene.

Instead, he grabbed the black robe off the wall and wrapped her in it. Although she struggled to get away, he scooped her in his arms, brought her over to the cushioned lounger and cradled her onto his lap.

"Dana, what's wrong? Did I hurt you?" He held her close against his chest. Feeling her body shake nearly broke his heart.

"No, Jack, you didn't hurt me. In fact, I enjoyed it. I don't know why I freaked all of a sudden. Just trapped I guess. I'm sorry."

Relieved, he chuckled as he stroked her hair. "No need to be sorry. That's why we have a safe word. Hold still, let me take the nipple clamps off. This might hurt a bit."

As he loosened the first clamp, she sucked in air. "Ow!"

"One more."

"Damn, that hurts."

"I think you might've reached subspace, and it scared you." He took off the other one and gently rubbed the circulation back into her sensitive tips. "Better?"

She nodded and leaned her head against his chest. "Subspace?"

"It's like a light trance. Your perception can be altered and it can be disorienting."

"That must explain it then." She frowned.

His guts twisted in knots. How the hell did he lose control of the scene? "You have to be honest with me. What was I doing, or what were you thinking that made you panic?"

She wasn't sure what happened. If she told Jack she thought she heard someone else in the dungeon, he might think she was crazy. It was probably her imagination. "Nothing." Squirming out of his lap, she stood, picked up her clothes from the chair and got dressed. "I didn't panic. It just got to be too much I guess. Maybe this lifestyle isn't right for me."

Jack didn't say anything for a moment. He pulled on his pants. "I disagree. I can tell by how you responded but that's something you have to decide for yourself. I think something else bothered you."

As he hung up the robe, she turned away and started up the stairs. "I have to go."

"Stop, Dana, hang on." He slipped on his shoes and chased after her, catching her halfway up the stairs. Turning her in his arms, he raised her chin. "Please tell me what happened." He saw fear in her eyes. What the hell went wrong?

"What are the black robes about? Why do the others go into the forest? Where are they going? I saw the robe in your closet. Are you in some kind of cult?" Her voice had a dream-like slur to it.

"It's not a cult."

"They looked like a bunch of Druids or something. It's pretty freaky."

He nodded. He was beginning to understand. "The robe spooked you."

"Yeah."

"The people in this town are very conservative, but they respect Celtic rituals. If they were to see people entering the woods in black robes, they wouldn't think twice."

"Is that what Damon, Shannon and the others are doing, Celtic rituals?"

"They're going to a private club in the forest called Dagda's Edge. It's like an invitation-only BDSM club. The robes hide their fetish outfits, which might cause some concern with the neighbors. Bad publicity for the dinner show. The robes are for privacy, nothing overly mysterious. Well maybe a little."

She let out a breath. "Have you been to this club?"

"Yes, once you've been there, you're welcome to return."

"Were you going to take me there?"

"If you were receptive to it." Why take their sessions beyond more than a sensual exploration? Dana would leave in a matter of weeks. Taking her to Dagda's Edge required a commitment that he didn't think either of them was ready for. He'd made that mistake before and the consequences devastated him and Cleona.

She glanced away, unable to meet his gaze. "Not now though." The sadness and disappointment in her voice were unmistakable.

"Maybe we went too fast. I know we've talked online, but we really don't know each other that well. It takes time to build trust." He gave her a hug. "Come on. Let me pack up and I'll take you back to your cottage."

She stood her ground. "So that's it? What if I want to try this again? What if I want to go to Dagda's Edge?"

"It's more intense than our scene in the dungeon. This lifestyle isn't for everyone and that's okay."

"No, it's not okay," she snapped at him. "I don't know enough about a D/s relationship yet. And I want to learn more."

"I've never had anyone...call a safe word before." He was going to say freak out during a session but held his tongue. "I should've seen your discomfort before it went too far. That's my fault, my failing. You don't know enough yet to know when to quit."

Concern creased her brow, then she smiled, put her arms around his neck and kissed him. "Thank you for being protective of me. Clearly I was aroused during the session. I just need us to try again."

He groaned. "We will then. If you can surrender as my sub, I'll help you find ecstasy beyond your wildest fantasies. You must trust me though."

"Will you take me to Dagda's Edge?" Although she was curious, the thought of a forbidden place even more wicked than the dungeon made her a bit nervous.

"No, you're not ready for Dagda's Edge." Maybe she was inexperienced in this lifestyle, but his words still stung.

She turned and started up the stairs.

"Dana, stop!"

She couldn't ignore the command in his voice. Turning around, she spoke calmly. "Jack, I'll trust you to make that decision but tonight I'd rather go to my cottage alone."

"That's fine, but I'm walking you back. Wait for me to pack up."

Her shoulders slumped and she sat down on the steps. "Okay. I'll wait."

Back in the dungeon, Jack stuffed all the sex toys and devices on the table into a duffel bag. He made sure everything was cleaned up. The fire would burn out soon, so that was safe, but not the fire burning within him. He knew he would be Dana's Master, if only she'd let go of her inhibitions. He pushed aside other thoughts that might be causing her fears and hesitations—like his own failing in past D/s relationships.

Damn it, he knew how to reach her. He could master her. Or was something holding him back too?

* * *

Moonlight brightened their path across the open field next to the castle. All the members of the troupe had left. A cool breeze rustled the dried grass. Chirps of crickets or other night creatures were the only sound. Jack pulled her close to his side and she drew in his warmth.

"Shannon said she'd ask around about the brooch. If no one claims it, she'll give it back to you."

"Thanks. It's a beautiful piece. I've grown attached to it."

Dana glanced into the forest behind the cottages. Lights flickered, first golden, then red, sending shadows through the tree branches. "Is there a road back there? I see lights. Or maybe a campfire?" she asked.

"No road and no fire," he said. "They could be from the Dagda's Edge."

"The others are there tonight again."

"Probably."

"Oh." She couldn't hide the disappointment in her tone. "Can't help thinking I'm missing out on something."

He took a breath. "It's more than a kink club. You have to have an open mind about ancient folklore and mystical ways. It's hard to explain."

"What folklore and mystical ways? Why are you being so evasive? Just tell me."

"It's best you learn things at a particular pace. It's better for you and those connected to the cottage. Can you trust me on this?"

"All right. But when I've learned what I need to, will you take me to Dagda's Edge?"

"If I think you're ready for it, I will, yes."

Dana opened the door to her cottage and let herself in. "Good night, Jack." As much as she'd like to spend the night with him, she needed some time alone to think.

"The night will be cold, let me start you a peat fire, then I'll say good night."

"Okay."

Jack knelt in front of her small fireplace and stacked sods of turf, sticks and starter and soon had a glowing fire burning. The heat took the chill out of her room. Dana turned on the light on the dresser and dropped her small purse on top. She starred at the Celtic pin sitting on top. "Does Shannon have a key to my cottage?" she asked.

Jack didn't look up. He still tended the fire, making sure it burned strong. "No, why would she have a key?"

"Don't know. I just found the brooch on my dresser."

"What?" He stood and strode over, stared down at it and frowned. "Don't know. Maybe she had Mr. Donegal let her in, but I don't understand why he'd do that. I guess it's yours."

"Great. It's a beautiful piece." Her voice betrayed a lack of enthusiasm. She'd about had enough of this game. She picked it up and a shiver raced through her body like an electric current. The room tilted and she grabbed Jack to keep from falling.

"Dana, are you all right?"

"I think so. Just a light vertigo." Then it hit her again and images flashed across her mind. A young man who she never met dressed in medieval clothing walked beside her as they entered a two-story stone house. She could smell a fire burning in the fireplace, the wild flowers in a wooden vase. Another flash and they lay naked on a bed, making love. And then two men dragged her through the woods while she kicked and screamed. They brought her to the edge of a bog and shoved her head under. Her lungs filled with water and muck. Struggling, she fought to breathe, get away, but the images faded to darkness.

"Dana!" Jack shook her. He cradled her in his arms on her bed. "Are you okay?"

Her lungs burned from the memory, but she breathed without effort. "I'm okay. What happened?"

"I think you fainted. But you screamed."

"You may think I'm crazy, but I think there's something odd about that brooch."

"How so?"

"Ever since I found it, odd things have happened."

He searched her face. Maybe he was trying to figure out if she was crazy, maybe thinking he needed to send her home.

"I'm sure it's nothing more than over-imagination. I'll let you know if it happens again."

CHAPTER THIRTEEN

End of Summer

Over the next couple weeks, Jack introduced Dana to many aspects of a D/s relationship. During their sessions and lovemaking, she discovered a deeper level of sensuality and pleasure she hadn't expected.

By the beginning of August, she considered the possibility of staying on in Ireland, but the email from her old boss caught her off guard. He'd asked her what day she'd expected to return to work. It dropped a gloomy shadow over her entire summer.

She'd been avoiding the actual decision of what she would do after the musician job ended. Safe and secure had always been her way, and now the email only made the decision harder. He offered her a raise and a new position if she returned as planned to her job in the security company by September first.

A text message from her friend Karen said she couldn't wait to see Dana or hear about her summer. As much as she loved Ireland and was falling for Jack, she was also feeling homesick. Was she like a kid on summer break trying to hang onto a foolish dream by considering relocating to Ireland? That was a huge decision and not very practical.

The idea of leaving Jack was painful but there wasn't much she could do. She had about a month before her return flight. Jack had offered suggestions on where she might find work, but the prospects weren't hopeful. The security company was the logical choice. Her father was right, performing as a harpist wasn't a real job, it was a hobby, something she should be proud of, but still a hobby, not something she could do as a career. She should stop acting like a gypsy and get her act together. She and Jack had a hot summer romance, nothing more.

"I see you didn't wear the brooch tonight," Jack said before the dinner show began. "You've worn it every night."

"No, I didn't. You may think I'm crazy, but strange things seem to happen when I wear it. I'll place it in my drawer, and later I'll find it in my jacket pocket, or pinned to a sweater. I tried leaving it in my cottage. Other strange things are happening too."

"I don't think you're crazy. Ireland is full of folklore and mystical stories. What kind of strange things?"

She shrugged. "I think the brooch has mystical powers. I keep having odd dreams, even when I'm awake."

"Hmmm." He frowned. "What kind of dreams?"

She shook her head. "Some are pleasant of a woman making love in an ancient home, but not the castle. Another dream is her running away from two men who finally catch her and drown her in the bog."

His eyes widened. "Maybe you shouldn't wear the pin anymore. It obviously disturbs you somehow."

"I don't feel good or bad energy when I touch it or wear it, except for that one time when I fainted and that one bad dream. Maybe the pin has a connection to the person who owned it, and I'm picking up her energy."

"This castle and its grounds are full of mystical energies. Just don't wear it and you won't have any problems."

After the dinner show, Dana bade the guests farewell as she usually did and snuck down into the dungeon to wait for her Master. The dungeon was a secret place for pleasure and pain. Jack had to arrange for them to take turns with the others in the troupe. Apparently the dungeon was a popular spot. And tonight she'd planned a little test of her own. She loved the strong, Dominant voice Jack used as he commanded her in sensual, reassuring ways through adventurous sexual games.

In the dungeon, she added another turf briquette to the fire already burning. With what she had planned, they might be there a while, if not all night. Undressing out of her costume, she got completely naked and slipped on the come-fuck-me red heels she'd bought in town and had stuffed in her purse. She untied her hair from the twist she wore for the show and let her brown waves drape over her shoulders and back. As usual, he had the table filled with hedonistic supplies.

There was something frightening and exciting about being restrained. Her arousal told her loud and clear that bondage added another dimension to sex, and she liked it. She was so turned on and Jack hadn't even arrived yet. She hoped tonight's session ended with him fucking her because she wanted to feel his hard cock thrusting inside her. The sound of footsteps on the stone steps made tremors course through her body. Quickly, she took the position on the slant bench, legs spread wide, ass high and her breasts resting on a padded board.

When he entered the dungeon, he said, "Mmmm. My sub is eager. Naked already and in position. I like the shoes."

"Thank you, Master. I wore them to please you."

He shed his Renaissance clothing and stood in front of her naked. His cock, hard and erect, swayed in front of her face, teasing her. Licking her lips, she was tempted to lean forward and take him into her mouth. "Why did you choose the bench? I had ordered you to stand by the wall restraints," he said as he moved closer and stroked her breasts, then gave her nipples a hard pinch, just enough to show his disappointment.

She gasped. His cock was an inch from her face. She could smell his musky scent but she didn't dare take him without permission. What she planned later was bad enough.

"Why did you disobey my command?" Shifting position, his hand slid over her ass, down her cleft, then he sank a finger into her cunt. "You're dripping."

"I didn't think of it as disobeying. I'm still trying to understand all this as I learn to trust and let go." Dana muffled a moan. "I chose the bench because I do love to be flogged, Master. And I'd hoped to suck your cock tonight and then feel you fuck me."

He gave a sexy, low laugh. "I like when my sub expresses her needs as long as she doesn't try to top from the bottom. Or maybe you're hoping I'll punish you more tonight."

"Yes, Master, if that's your wish."

"My sub should trust me more. If she would surrender herself completely, her pleasure would be greater."

"I do trust you, Master."

"Not completely. Get up and stand by the wall like I'd asked." His words were firm but gentle. Stretching her arms straight up over her head and spreading her legs wide apart, he strapped her into the shackles that were anchored into the wall and floor. "Comfortable?"

"Yes, Master." Anticipation made her pussy twitch and her nipples harden, erect and sensitive, aching for his touch or the sting of the nipple clamps. Her eyes drifted over to the hammock suspended from the ceiling, the one where Shannon had writhed and screamed in pure pleasure. She didn't believe she'd yet reached that level of ecstasy that Shannon had.

Jack lifted her chin and brought his face close. "Where are your thoughts, my lady?"

"I was remembering Shannon for a moment."

Jack let out a breath then squeezed her nipple until she yelped. "Keep your thoughts here and you'll enjoy this much more." He unshackled her ankles and turned her around to face the wall, then reshackled her ankles. "Extra punishment should keep you focused." He stroked her cheek, his gaze so intent on her face. Then he laid his mouth on hers, teased her lips with his tongue, and kissed her with a passion she had never anticipated. Her body melted, heated thoroughly to her toes. When he ended the kiss she moaned. She wanted more, wanted to wrap her arms around him and draw him close. The pleasure both consumed and intoxicated her.

"Yes, please, Master."

He began with the flogger, swatting her buttocks and thighs and gently stroking the sides of her breasts. The rough, cool stone rubbed against her nipples and heightened their sensitivity. Rocking her hips, she ached to rub her clit against something to ease the throbbing. If he touched her there, she could come with little effort. The flogging stopped and she caught herself before she groaned out loud.

"We're going to try something different tonight." She heard him pick up something from the table but didn't turn her head to look. His rough hand rubbed her ass then she felt a sharp sting on one side.

She cried out from the sharp pain. "What was that, Master?"

"A cane." Swat! He struck her again on the other side and the sting rang through her body. Clenching her teeth, she waited as the pain converted to waves of throbbing between her legs. Her pulse pounded in her head. She hoped she'd feel another strike because her body hummed.

Swat! Swat! Her body jerked and she groaned. Her hips and knees quivered as her groin craved attention. His mouth, fingers or any stimulation would send her over into a blissful orgasm.

He stopped and rubbed her ass, then slipped toward her pussy. "Edge," she cried out.

He pulled his hand away. "Very good. I hadn't given you permission to come." He put the cane down and picked up something else. When he returned, he worked her nipples between his thumb and forefinger and attached nipple clamps.

Manipulating her already raw and sensitive nipples pushed her to the brink of another orgasm. What if she ignored his order and allowed herself to come? Would he give her more punishment? Maybe then she'd reach that level of ecstasy like Shannon.

"Is my slave's mind drifting again?"

"No, Master. I liked the cane."

He gave a short laugh. "I could tell. You like the clamps too."

"Yes, they feel good."

Sliding his hand between her legs, he thrust a finger inside her and pressed his hard cock against her tender buttocks. Dana rocked her hips as he fucked her with his finger. She wanted more. She wanted his thick cock filling her.

"Wet, yes. But I don't think you're quite ready." His hand slipped from her body and he moved to the table. A moment later the cane struck her again and again.

Instantly, her pussy clenched. Her clit was so hard, it ached. "How about now?" Sliding his hand around, she knew the moment he touched her she would come, but she didn't warn him this time or fight to hold back.

His fingers stroked her swollen and sensitive clit and she plunged over the edge in an intense orgasm. "Master, I can't stop it. I'm coming."

CHAPTER FOURTEEN

Pain and Pleasure

"Fuck." Jack dropped the cane and pressed his body to her, stroking her clit until the tremors of her orgasm eased. Why hadn't she warned him sooner? It happened, especially to a novice, but they'd been together for weeks now. After the spasms from her body ceased, he left her shackled and didn't say a word. As much as he wanted to fuck her, he had to give her a punishment for defying him.

Walking over to the table, he picked up a black scarf and returned slowly. Dana strained to look over her shoulder to see what he was doing, her eyes wide. He blindfolded her, then left her there. Long moments passed. She kept lifting her head as if trying to hear what he was doing but he remained very still. When her body started to tremble, he began pacing the room so she'd hear him walking, then he shoved the lounger. The noise made her jump.

"Master? I'm sorry, I didn't let you know. I was testing you."

He squeezed his eyes shut and didn't answer. Not good.

Damn, she was so beautiful, and so innocent, it was killing him to do this. When she whimpered, he thought his heart would break but he bit his lip. "It wasn't the orgasm, it was the fact that you did it to defy me. I can't have a sub 'testing' me. Either you trust me or you don't." Her safety was in his hands.

"Testing may have been the wrong word. And I wasn't trying to anger you. I'm trying to understand all aspects of this type of relationship. I trust you, I feel safe with you. I just don't understand all of it yet."

He relaxed a bit. He couldn't argue her logic. As an intelligent woman, she was carefully evaluating this lifestyle. He couldn't fault her for that. He picked up a crop, stood by the lounger, and swatted the brocade material to bring her back to his attention, his control. Dana jumped and cried out from the sharp crack. He then slipped on a condom and approached her.

Without a word he unshackled her ankles, and Dana attempted to turn around. He pressed her against the wall to keep her back to him. She didn't protest. When she tried to squeeze her legs together, he roughly pushed them apart. His commands were by touch, and she followed his orders without hesitation.

Legs spread and arms over her head, Dana remained quiet until he struck her with the crop on her buttocks. She let out a yelp and her body jerked. Her breathing quickened. The crop glided up and down each leg, to her pussy, up her back, over her breasts, then arms, like a gentle caress, a tease, then slowly back down and rested on her buttocks. He gave her another swat. She yelped. Her body quivered. God damn, he wanted to take her now, but his lesson wasn't over yet.

Sliding his hand between her legs, he felt her cream soaking her pussy. She was ready for him.

He struck her again, not as hard because he saw she was slumping in the restraints. She never moved her legs even without the shackles. Good slave. His cock hardened and his balls tightened; he didn't know how much longer he could stand not taking her. Finally, her groans of pleasure were too much of a temptation. His slave loved pain so much—maybe too much—and he didn't want to overdo it. Had he brought out more than her submissive side? Did Dana have desires of a masochist? That was a whole other challenge he'd consider later. Right now, he had to be inside her.

Dropping the crop, he spun her around and lifted her legs to wrap around his hips and plunged deep inside her.

"Omigod," she cried out.

Her hands gripped around the chains that held her to the wall as he drove his cock rapidly into her. The sight of the nipple clamps on her distended peaks drove him deeper and harder with his thrusts. Tightening her legs around his hips, she let out a groan that told him she was coming again. He felt the pressure build, then let out a bellow as his orgasm exploded inside her.

When the pulsing eased, he slid out of her, unfastened the shackles, wrapped her in a blanket from the table and took her into his arms. He brought her to the lounger and sat her down. After discarding the condom, he brought her a damp cloth from the table of supplies. Pulling her onto his lap, he gently removed the nipple clamps.

"Ouch. They always hurt worse coming off." She gave a chuckle.

"So I've heard."

She held him close and looked at him, giving him a tentative smile. "I had another reason, Master." There was no defiance in her voice. The gentleness in her eyes twisted in his gut.

"Why, Dana? I know you're still learning, but you're not a novice anymore. You've always told me when you were close before, but this time I think you defied me on purpose."

"Not to anger you, but I wanted to be punished, punished harder."

He studied her for a moment. "It's more than that. Tell me."

"I think you hold back. I wanted to disobey an order to receive a more severe punishment to see if..."

"To see if what?" His words were sharper than he'd intended.

"If extreme pain would bring the ecstasy that Shannon experienced that first day I arrived."

He shook his head. "No, love. It has nothing to do with the level of pain. Something else is holding you back. Lack of trust, fear. I don't know. I bring you right to the point where I think you'll completely surrender and then you backpedal. You hesitate for some reason. A lack of communication between a Master and his sub can be dangerous. I'm responsible for your safety."

"I know." She nodded and rested her head on his chest. "Jack, I'm leaving in less than a month. I'm running out of time."

"Maybe that's it. You're thinking about leaving. You're afraid to get too close." He pulled her back to look into her eyes. "Stay then. You can live with me. I'll help you find some kind of work, maybe where you can play your harp."

She shook her head. "I have a good job at home. There's no guarantee here."

"Who said life has guarantees? Follow your heart."

The emotion in her eyes surprised him. "Why don't you come back to the states with me?"

He shook his head. "I can't. I just signed the loan to buy my uncle's store yesterday. If I were to sell it, he wouldn't have any place to work. Since my aunt died, working is the only thing that gives him joy. I can't take that away from him."

"I understand." The sad tone in her voice broke his heart. "You're a kind person to do that."

"It's not a sacrifice to take care of those we love." He hugged her closer. "What gives you joy?"

She considered that for a moment. "You. My harp."

He took her face in his hands and kissed her, slow, deep and sensual. Then kissed her forehead. How would he say good-bye to her when the time came? She'd leave him like Cleona had left him. "Dana, stay here with me. We can work out the details together. I want more than a sexual submissive. I want you."

Her heart was breaking. Did she love him? Maybe but she didn't want to give him any promises she couldn't keep. "I don't know if it's possible. I'll have to think about it."

"Do that. Like you said, you don't have much time." He rose, got dressed and began packing his devices and toys in a duffel.

She dressed and started up the stairs.

"Wait, I'll walk you back," he said.

"I can find my way." She continued walking.

"I know, but I'm walking you back. Wait."

She came back down and sat on the lounger.

Returning to the table, Jack stuffed the rest of the items into the bag. *My slave needs to trust me.* He was about to shut off the lights when he noticed a piece of metal on the table next to his duffel. A cold shiver went up his back. It wasn't there a moment ago. He didn't want to touch it. Finally, he picked up the intricate brooch and turned it over. It looked much like the one Dana always wore. But it couldn't be the same one.

"I thought you said you didn't wear the brooch tonight," he said.

"I didn't. It's in my dresser drawer in the cottage."

"Isn't this it?" He held it in the palm of his hand.

"Yes, but how did you get it?"

"It was on the table."

"Someone playing a prank?" she asked.

He knew the troupe wouldn't do that. "No, it's not a prank, it's a message. I believe it's an invitation, like a key." Jack stared at the brooch, then stuffed it in his duffel. If he was wrong, he'd be opening himself to the risk of pain and loss all over again. Was Dana ready to cross that threshold? Was he? Their sessions had been hot, exploring the D/s world, and Dana roleplaying as his sub and slave. He'd sworn he wouldn't take it to the next step, knowing she would be leaving at the end of the summer. More than taking their D/s play into a more serious level, he wasn't ready to let himself go, feel something deeper.

Even now, he remembered the turmoil with Cleona. The intensity of their relationship and how their love bound them together, but the conflicts of her commitments and her regrets tore them apart. It had killed him to let her go.

"An invitation for what?"

"You've been invited to Dagda's Edge."

* * *

When Dana got back to her cottage, she boiled water and added it to the teapot, then changed out of her medieval costume into a tee-shirt and jeans. It was late and she should try to sleep, but doubted sleep would come. Jack had said he needed to finish some paperwork for his uncle's shop, so he'd gone to his cottage. Just as well. She needed time to think. The idea of visiting Dagda's Edge excited her.

The mystique surrounding the place raised her curiosity. Now she'd find out what it was all about. She worried more about the big decision she had to make. Could she possibly consider moving to Ireland with Jack? There was more to consider than just moving into a guy's place. Giving up her job, moving to another country, finding another job, leaving friends and family behind, and what if it didn't work out?

After the discussion with Jack she should be pouring herself a large goblet of mead. The herbal tea was a better choice. The mead would make her a bit daft and she needed a clear head to sort out her troubles. As she hung up her costume, the brooch dropped to the floor. Hadn't Jack placed the pin inside his duffel? The brooch almost had a mind of its own, as if trying to show off its supernatural powers. She believed there was some type of magic going on and it didn't frighten her. The meaning didn't make sense. Perhaps accepting the possibilities of a mystical presence around the castle was the whole point.

She laughed. She'd show it to Jack. He'd remember about placing the brooch in his bag. Magical pin in hand, she ran over to his cottage and knocked on his door. No answer. "Jack? You there?" No answer. There weren't any lights on inside either. Odd. She returned to her cottage, tossed the pin in her drawer, then placed a kettle on the stove to heat water. She took a teacup from the cupboard.

When she was about to pour hot water into it, she found the brooch sitting inside the cup. She cried out and nearly dropped the kettle.

Slamming it down on the stove, she looked around her room. "Hello? Jack? Are you in here?" She checked under the bed, in the bathroom and closet but there was no sign of him. Next she went outside again and over to

Jack's cottage. Still no light inside. What was going on with this piece of old jewelry?

She'd find out. Back inside her cottage, she put on her jacket, pinned the brooch to it, grabbed a flashlight and marched outside, straight into the forest. Behind her she could see the lights from the castle so she wouldn't get lost. By following the direction she remembered seeing the others in robes take, she expected to eventually find the club.

After stepping into soft, spongy earth and around trees, she discovered a narrow path. The lights from the cottages and the castle glowed dimly through the trees behind her. Directly in front of her, another light glowed. A large, two-story, stone building with a thatched roof stood in a small clearing. As she approached the house, a large, red door opened revealing a woman in a low-cut black dress and a festive party mask.

At first, Dana had the urge to turn around and run, but the woman beckoned her to approach with the wave of her hand. "Hello, Dana, please come in. We're pleased that you found us."

"How do you know me?"

"Jack told us about you. Although we expected you to arrive with Jack."

"I thought so too. But I couldn't find him, so I came alone. I want to know what Dagda's Edge is all about."

The woman chuckled. "Well, that depends on what you're looking for. It can be an escape, a potent source of pleasure and exploration, an obsession, a place for fun and merriment, or a curse. This home was built in the 15th Century on the intersection of two powerful ley lines. It's also a doorway to other dimensions and times."

"Other dimensions and times? Seriously?" Dana returned, giving the woman a disbelieving glare. "That's a little farfetched."

"How do you explain your recent dreams or Dagda's gift?"

"How do you know about my dreams? And what gift?" Dana asked.

"That brooch you be wearing." The woman pointed to Dana's right side. The brooch was pinned to her jacket. "It's your invitation. And the brooch is known to influence the wearer's dreams."

Dana gasped, but wasn't that surprised. "Jack did say we were invited. Is Dagda a person or a place? Are you Dagda?"

"No, I'm not Dagda, but he is a person. Come inside and I'll explain."

CHAPTER FIFTEEN

Dagda's Edge

L ight flickered from a large fireplace in the main room off of a kitchen. Warmth from the fire and the welcoming scents of herbs and incense eased Dana's mind. Whispered voices and the thumping of music drifted down from upstairs rooms. The furnishings appeared antique in style but looked brand new, with brocade chairs and sofas trimmed in carved wood.

"Please sit, Dana. I'll have Adara bring us some refreshments."

Dana sat in a large chair by the fire and realized how late it was, almost midnight. "I'm so sorry to have disturbed you this late. I can come back another time."

"Not at all. We're open all the time, when the lines are in proper alignment we're here."

Dana frowned at the last remark. She didn't quite understand what she meant.

The woman smiled sympathetically. "It'll all make sense to you soon. I'm Dru. Forgive me for not introducing myself sooner. I'm the caretaker of Dagda's Edge. Sort of the manager too." Dru removed her mask. Her cobalt blue eyes shone in the fire and her long, black hair draped across the middle of her back. Shorter wisps of hair framed her face and brought attention to high cheekbones and smooth skin. She was that indeterminate age of somewhere between early thirties and late forties. The long, black dress accentuated her curvy figure...not slim, not voluptuous, but very sensuous. Her nails were trimmed and painted with a dark, plum polish.

"Nice to meet you."

"We knew you would come with or without Jack. Sometimes a member invites a lover or friend to the cottage. But it was different with you."

"How so?"

"Dagda's Edge invited you."

Dana gave a nervous laugh. "What? That doesn't make sense."

"Besides the energy from the ley lines, the cottage itself has mystical powers that it has collected over the centuries. Some are drawn to that energy like you. Dagda's Edge was named after the folktale Dagda's harp. A harp that when struck, had the power to make an enemy warrior cry, laugh and sleep, allowing Dagda to escape with his harp. This cottage has many powers."

"It's odd that you call it a cottage," Dana said. "It's more like a large house to me. How did this place acquire these powers?"

Dru smiled. "In the 15th Century, Rogan Magartan, Earl of Coghlan, had a mistress and he built Dagda's Edge as their private sanctuary in the forest. The woman he was betrothed to, and later married, was a bitter woman from a powerful neighboring clan. She discovered Rogan's lover. Friends connected to the cottage helped the mistress escape to another time and dimension. But guilt and longing for her lover, Rogan, forced her to return. Only to meet with a tragic end. Rogan's wife had men from her clan capture Cleona MacCormack the moment she left Dagda's Edge. Cleona was discovered drowned in the bogs near the castle."

Dana sat straighter in her chair. "Isn't Cleona the name of Jack's last girlfriend?"

"Yes." Dru didn't give further explanation. Dana turned the possibilities over in her mind.

A tall, slim redhead strolled into the room carrying a silver tray with a teapot, cups and a plate of sliced nut bread. She wore a short black leather dress, trimmed in red lace and her hair was razor cut and angled at her jaw. How she walked steady in the high, pencil-thin heels, Dana didn't know.

She placed the tray on a side table and looked at Dana. Her eyes widened. "Oh, my. It's you. I'm so glad you're back." Tears filled the redhead's eyes.

"You must have me confused with someone else," Dana said. "This is my first time here."

"This is Dana Brennan from America. She plays the folk harp in the minstrel dinner show. Dana this is Adara." Dru stood and poured cream in the tea cups, then prepared tea and handed a cup to Dana.

"But she's wearing the brooch," Adara argued.

"Cleona left it behind," Dru said. "I gave it to Dana as a gift. I sensed she should have it."

"You gave the brooch to me?" It didn't make much sense why a stranger would give her a gift, but Jack did say it was an invitation.

Dru nodded.

"Thank you, it's beautiful," Dana said, then turned to Adara. "Who did you think I was?"

"My mistake," Adara said. "Would you like a slice of nut bread?"

"Yes, please." Dana thought it would be rude to refuse. "I love your accent. It's different from any I've heard so far. May I ask where you're from?"

"Adara works for Dagda's Edge. She's been with us for several years," Dru offered. "Where she's from will take some explanation."

Adara wiped away tears. "Sorry. Dana reminds me of a friend I hadn't seen in a while."

"Yes, there is a resemblance." Dru sat with her tea and took a sip. "Adara came to us escaping a tormented life. Here she found a home and discovered that she craved the sexual rush of the BDSM lifestyle as a slave. There were many Doms, both male and female, willing to train her and pleasure her. But Adara also discovered her need to express her dominant side and is now a switch."

"I'm glad you're here, Dana," Adara said. "I have work to do, but I hope to see you later. I'd love to tell you about where I'm from. I hope we'll be friends."

"That would be nice." Dana turned to Dru. "Everyone who comes here is into BDSM?"

Dru took a sip before answering. "Mostly, but it's more than that. We're like an oasis or a refuge for those who desire other sensual pleasures, and also need to discover a deeper knowledge about life and themselves. How long have you known that you were a submissive?"

"What? Who put you up to this? Did Jack or Shannon say something?" Her voice shook with anger. How dare this stranger ask these personal questions?

"You would not have received an invitation, unless you were ready to explore your deepest desires, face the fears in your life. I always ask questions about new arrivals." Her voice was firm, yet compassionate. "Don't you want to understand your desires? Don't you have questions about who you are and what you want to do with your life?"

A lump formed in Dana's throat and tears filled her eyes. All of this was true. She did want to figure this out. "Yes, I do."

"Are you a sub or a Domme?"

"A sub."

"Very well. We will provide whatever assistance you need when you return. Do you have something sexy to wear? A club outfit, preferably leather?" She rose to lead her out the front door.

"I have a leather skirt. I bought it at Jack's shop and a tank."

"That will do. Get changed into that. I'll come to your cottage shortly to escort you to Dagda's Edge."

"Should I contact Jack? Shouldn't we come here together?"

"No, I have selected a Master specifically for you. You have many obstacles to overcome, before you're ready for complete surrender and joy. Your questions will be answered, your needs met. You can continue to deny your true nature and be miserable, or sense there is something missing, or you can come to the cottage with me and let the Master help you break down the barriers."

"Barriers? Obstacles?" She hadn't thought about that. "Is this safe?"

"Completely. I can stay with you the whole time if you wish."

CHAPTER SIXTEEN

Altered Time

Dana ran to Jack's cottage and pounded on his door. It was well past midnight. His cottage was dark, and he didn't answer. Maybe he'd gone into town to stay at the store? She doubted it, because his car was parked in front of the cottages right next to her rental. Damn. Where the hell was he? Was she finally going to Dagda's Edge, but alone without him?

Back in her place she quickly changed into the black leather skirt, a midnight-blue shimmery tank and strappy black heels. As soon as she finished dressing, a knock at her door made her jump. She had to take a couple breaths before she had the nerve to open the door.

"Shannon!"

"Ready to go?" Shannon smiled. She wore one of those black robes and had another robe draped over her arm. She glanced down at her shoes. "You'll have to carry those and wear something you can walk in through the forest."

"You're my escort?"

Shannon nodded. "Hurry up, the Master is waiting."

"Who's the Master? I don't feel right about this. What about Jack?"

Shannon continued smiling. "Jack would approve. You're in training and you'll love Dagda's Edge. Put this on first." Shannon handed her a black hooded robe.

Outside there was no breeze, and the sounds of the crickets and frogs had stopped. Dana's heart pounded, taking her breath away. What was she getting into? If only Jack was with her. "Shouldn't we find Jack and ask him to come?"

"Follow me." Shannon led her into the forest. "You're doing the right thing."

After a few minutes, Dana saw the golden glow of lights through the trees, that same strange glow she'd seen before. She and Shannon passed through two stone pillars and an open wrought-iron gate. A coiled Celtic knot decorated the center of the gate. The motif was bent and rusted. How beautiful it must've been when first made.

The level of excitement almost overwhelmed her. I can do this. Her hands grabbed fistfuls of the robe as they walked closer to the building. At the end of the walkway was the large stone house with a thatched roof. Dagda's

Edge. This time she noticed there was no parking lot, or driveway, no cars, just forest. She couldn't see any road that led to the house.

"It's a beautiful old place. And much larger inside than it looks." Shannon showed her to the entrance, a large man stood at the red door. He nodded and opened the weathered wooden door for them. "This is Hayden," Shannon explained. "If there's any trouble, Hayden will handle it. But you won't have any problems. You're safe here." Hayden remained at the door like a human brick wall.

Inside Dana was stunned. Was her mind playing tricks? The cozy antique cottage had completely changed. The furnishings took a surreal transformation resembling a luxurious hotel with polished woods, overstuffed leather chairs and couches. An elegant bar and smoky tables stood at one side of the large room, and hallways led off from the main area. Sensual music with a steady beat played in the background. Soft candlelight flickered from tables and the bar. The air was heavy with spicy scented candles, leather and sex.

Women dressed in scanty leather and lace, boots or heels, strolled the room or leaned against men who wore leather or black trousers and black shirts or no shirts. A few guests strolled the elegant room naked or close to it. "We have something here for everyone's taste. I'm sure you'll find what you're looking for."

Shannon removed her robe and took Dana's sneakers and handed them to a petite woman at the door. Dana put on her strappy heels. "I'll hold these until you're ready to leave," the woman with several facial piercings and black, spiky hair said. She wore a black lace body stocking that left nothing to the imagination with outrageously high platform heels.

Dru approached them, holding her hand out to Dana. "Hello, Dana. Welcome back. So glad to have you here." She shook Dana's hand. Dana admired her sexy, black dress, more seductive than what she'd worn earlier. The V in the front came down to her navel and the hem barely covered her ass. She also wore thigh-high boots.

"Thanks, I'm still a little confused." Dana noticed Kevin and Thea, two of the entertainers from the dinner show, at a table by the bar. Kevin wore only a leather vest and a collar around his neck. He was bent over the table as Thea held his leash and whipped him playfully with a cane. Each crack of the cane sent chills up Dana's spine.

Kevin's cock hardened and swayed with each strike.

At the far side of the room a woman was hung upside down, her legs spread slightly and her arms bound behind her back while her Dom held a large vibrator at her sex. The woman moaned and writhed.

Dru smiled, not giving the hedonistic display a second glance. "Dagda's Edge is a special place. There's something here for everyone like I told you. Those who enter the cottage may also cross time and dimensions. Make sure you're escorted before you leave."

That thought gave her a chill. What if she left without an escort? "Are you from another time or dimension, Dru?" Dana straightened and attempted to take all this in stride. How much of the mystical theory did she believe? She couldn't deny the strange events that had happened.

"No. The current time is my time. Adara is from the 15th Century. She came with Cleona, but Cleona could not adjust. Adara is quite happy here."

"Why was she crying before?"

"You remind her of her friend who was lost to her."

"I'm sorry I brought a sad memory to her." Dana hated being the cause of anyone's sadness. "Shannon said something about training?"

"By the time you leave, your questions will be answered. You're troubled by your relationship and have a few big decisions to make."

Dru's brutal honesty stabbed at Dana's heart. "Yes, you sound like a fortuneteller."

"Not at all. I'm just well informed. If you want your answers follow me. But first a lesson in trust." Dru walked over to the girl who had taken their robes and was handed something that looked like a masquerade mask. She came to Dana and handed it to her. "Put this on. It's a blindfold. When you can't see, you have to trust other senses."

Dana glanced at the mask in her hands, hesitating.

"It's all right, Dana," Shannon said. "Hurry, the Master waits."

"But what about Jack?"

"You love him, don't you?" Shannon asked, with a reassuring smile.

"Yes." She realized she'd never told Jack.

"And you want to break down the barriers between you two."

Dana nodded, staring at the mask.

"Then Jack would want you here."

CHAPTER SEVENTEEN

Love Lesson

Dana put the mask on. The eye holes were covered so she couldn't see. Then Dru and Shannon led her down a long hallway. Shannon was right, the cottage seemed much larger from the inside. The cracks of whips and moans and an occasional chain rattled as she walked down the hallway. They stopped then and she heard a door open. They led her inside. She felt so helpless not being able to see. The familiar smell of a turf fire filled the room, as well as the scent of leather and an incense other herb, eucalyptus. Just the smell of leather immediately made her aroused.

"Did you want Shannon to stay, Dana?" Dru asked.

"Yes," Dana answered.

"The Master says no, it's not necessary," Dru said. "Safe words here are 'red' and 'slow'. Understand, Dana?"

"Yes." Panic set in. Did this Master expect to have sex with her? "Shannon? Jack would agree to this? I mean, I know I have things to learn about the D/s lifestyle, but this can't be right me being with someone else."

"Jack would approve, Dana," Shannon said. "You want to understand what's holding you back, right?"

"Yes."

"We'll be leaving you now. You'll be fine," Shannon said. Dana heard the door close and rough hands gripped her and drew her across the room and up against the wall.

"Can you tell me what we're going to do, Master? I'm very nervous." Since Dru and Shannon referred to him as Master, she had better too. "I'm fairly new to this and Jack, my Master, wishes for me to live with him and not return to the states. That's a big decision, I—"

Pressing his fingertips over her lips, he signaled her to be silent. Then he raised her arms and clamped them into shackles. Dana gasped. He shoved her feet apart and secured them into a spreader bar. She still wore clothes. Would this experience with this Master help her to break down any remaining resistance she had with Jack so she could completely surrender to him? Would this also help with her decision to stay or return home? The Master stroked her cheek with his knuckles. If he'd only talk to her maybe this would be easier. Every inch of her body shook partly from fear and partly from anticipation.

She kept reminding herself that this Master was trained and she was doing this for Jack and herself. Right now, her body shook and muscles tensed as she heard the Master moving around a few feet away. The first crack of a flogger made her jump. Her cream flowed but she also tensed since it wasn't Jack. The flogger stuck the wall close to her but never touched her. How could the Master help her?

Moments later, the sound of chains replaced the cracks of the flogger and he released her arms and ankles, but shackled her wrists in cuffs and chains and walked her over to a chair. The heat from the fire warmed her flushed skin and calmed her. He pressed something to her mouth and at first she resisted. The thought of a ball gag made her cringe. "Master, I know I shouldn't speak, but if you gag me we haven't discussed safe signals."

He pressed his fingers to her lips to silence her, and she nodded. Then the object was at her mouth again. It was cool and she opened. He popped it in and she rolled it around in her mouth and bit down. The juice was sweet and squirted over her tongue. A grape. She giggled.

This time another piece with bumps, a raspberry? And several blueberries, then a spoonful of honey. The sweet syrup dripped down her chin and he lapped it up with his tongue. The first intimate touch made her stiffen but she didn't protest. In the back of her mind, she was still worried about where this would eventually lead. She truly loved Jack, she knew that for sure now and she didn't want to be with another man. Still, she was confused.

Tenderly the Master brushed her hair back and stroked the nape of her neck. It felt nice but she wished it was Jack. Images of their weeks together rushed through her mind; all wonderful times but always with the heavy feeling of knowing each day brought her closer to the time she would have to leave him. Tears flooded her eyes and dripped down her cheeks. And now she knew why she couldn't surrender to Jack.

The Master gently brushed her tears away. Then his fingers roamed down her neck to her shoulder and over to the side of her breast. Dana squirmed. Sensations coiled into a knot in her stomach and the tension spread through her muscles. "Red!"

The Master pulled his hand away. "Why are you crying, my lady?" It was Jack's voice.

"Jack!" Her heart leapt.

He lifted her mask and smiled.

"Because I know why I haven't been able to surrender to you completely." She quickly glanced around the room. It could've been any upscale hotel room with a bed and door to a bathroom except for the eyehooks on the ceiling and floor, various chains and straps hanging from them and also a table of bondage devices and sex toys.

He knelt in front of her looking so hot in leather pants and no shirt, his chest gleaming in the firelight. "Are you going to let out the secret?"

"Because I love you."

He smiled, then frowned. "Then why can't you surrender to me, trust me?"

"If I love you and surrender to you as your slave, it will be unbearably painful to leave you."

"Don't think about tomorrow or next week or leaving. You'll make the right decision when the time comes. Surrender to me tonight. Just tonight."

She relaxed a little. "Okay, just tonight." She let out a breath.

He undid the shackles around her wrists and ankles. "Undress for me, slave, but leave your shoes on. I like the heels."

Heat traveled to Dana's pussy as she unzipped her short skirt and let it drop to the floor. She hadn't worn panties so she stepped out of the skirt and kicked it aside. After pulling the tank over her head, she tossed it by her skirt. Completely naked except for her five-inch heels, she felt exposed and aroused under his inspection. When he removed his shoes and leather pants, her heart nearly stopped. Standing naked, he was so gorgeous, every hard muscle outlined, his hard cock, ready to satisfy her beyond her imagination.

"Good, slave. Will you submit to me tonight?"

"Yes, Master."

"Show me." His words held her in place with his commanding tone, but she wasn't sure what he wanted her to do. The walls in her vagina fluttered with need. She wanted to please him but how?

"I don't understand, Master."

"Show me that you will surrender and completely submit to me tonight. Show me."

After a panicked moment of hesitation, she walked up to him and knelt down.

She bowed her head in submission. Her face was inches from his cock. The temptation to take him in her mouth was strong but she waited for his permission.

"Yes," he breathed with a ragged breath. Lifting her chin, he gazed into her eyes. "My beautiful slave, I'm going to pleasure you and fuck you until you beg me to stop."

She smiled and glanced longingly at his cock.

He laughed. "You'd like to suck me first."

"Yes, Master."

"Take me into your mouth, but just for a moment."

"Thank you, Master." Running her tongue up and down his rigid shaft, she took him into her mouth and cradled his scrotum with her hand. He held her head, guiding her up and down. His groans rewarded her, and she loved the musky male and soap scent of him. When she released his shaft, she moved to his balls, gently sucking one into her mouth, and rolled her tongue around it. Taking his cock into her mouth again, she slid down to the base in quick thrusts. Pleasuring her Master gave her joy. Hearing his groans warmed her inside. A salty drop of pre-cum slipped from his slit and she lapped at it, wanting more.

His fingers tightened around her head as he thrust his cock, matching her rhythm, faster and faster, then abruptly pulled away from her. "God, that's so good. But I have to stop," he groaned. He drew her up to her feet, embraced her and kissed her deeply, held her close for a long time. "I love you, Dana. More than you'll ever know. Trust me, I will take care of you, my slave."

"Yes, Master."

"Now over to the swing."

She did and waited. Would he flog her first? Probe her ass with a butt plug? She shivered anticipating the unknown.

"Hands behind your back," he ordered. She obeyed, and he pinched her nipples, sucked them and grazed them with his teeth. Then he attached clamps to the distended tips. The nipples were still raw and sensitive from earlier but the pressure and sting made her clit throb and swell.

"That feels good, Master. I liked that very much. I like what you do to me, how I feel so intensely loved. It's a deliberate and powerful loving.

"There are many things in a Master/slave relationship we could explore." He sat her in the swing, then attached the straps to her wrists and ankles, adjusting the rigging so her arms and legs spread and pointed upward. This gave her Master access to her pussy and ass. "But tonight it's going to be about your threshold of pain and pleasure and trust. You seem to be obsessed with pain and to respond well to it. Still I don't want you to hesitate to tell me when something becomes too much."

"I promise, Jack."

"Good. I think I know why you crave the pain. It's more than what you saw Shannon experience." He kissed her then gave a swat on her ass with his hand. She yelped and giggled.

"Why?"

"Let's see if you can discover that yourself." Picking up another device from the table, he unwrapped a condom and slipped it over a dildo and applied some lubricant. When he brought it to her she noticed the straps. Spreading her labia, he gently worked the dildo into her channel and secured the straps around her waist to keep it in place. Then he turned it on. The vibrations sent shudders of sensations through her body and her clit began to swell and throb. Even her nipples throbbed as all her nerve endings came alive.

His fingertips rubbed her clit until she was about to shout out "edge" but then he stopped and picked up the flogger.

"Do not climax until I give you permission, slave."

"Yes, Master," she answered him through clenched teeth. She wasn't going to last long like this.

The flogger struck her ass in repeated strikes and her body quivered as she absorbed the pain and it transferred into pleasure. She moaned. Several more times and between her legs. "Edge!" she cried out.

He stopped the flogger and turned the vibrator down but not off. "Don't come. Hold it."

She was on the brink of an orgasm, but she held back. A moment later he switched the vibrator to high again and swatted her with a paddle. That hurt a lot. She was still tender from earlier lashings and each strike shot waves of sensations throughout her body. She cried out with each smack but didn't ask him to stop. Her hands gripped the straps and tightened as she tried to control her climax. So close.

Her clit throbbed and her pulse thumped in her head. Two more smacks and the thickness of the dildo in her cunt would push her to a sweet release. "Edge, Master. Edge." The words were harder to get out.

She tried focusing on something other than the vibrations in her cunt, the sharp pinching of her nipples, then felt a sharp swat on her ass. It was a cane, not the paddle. This hurt the worst. But good too. The pain absorbed into her body and turned to pleasure, an odd sensation that disconnected her from the physical world. She felt as if she was a feather drifting on a warm breeze. When the cane hit her the third time, her whole body hovered in the swing, aching for release. "Master," she breathed. "Edge. No strength left."

He stopped. "I need to be inside you."

"Yes, Master."

He removed the vibrator and then put on a condom. "But I'm going to fuck your beautiful ass tonight."

"Yes, Master." But her words held a tone of doubt. What if she couldn't do this?

"Relax, this is all about pleasure. I won't hurt you."

He lapped at her slit, his tongue worked her clit, bringing her closer to climax. "Soon, you'll have more pleasure than you can stand." His hands grasped her breasts and tugged at the nipple clamps. She moaned and wriggled in the restraints.

"Oh yes, Master. That's so good."

Bending lower, he coated his finger with water-soluble lubricant and circled her anus with his finger. Gently, he pressed slowly through the ring of muscle. She tightened with the initial pain.

"Easy, slave, breathe easy, relax. That's it." He slid in deeper and moved in and out slowly. "How does that feel?"

"Burned and hurt a little before. Feels good now." With his encouraging words and gentle movements, she relaxed a bit. The idea of taking his large cock like this made her nervous but also excited her.

Then he slid two fingers in a little at a time. She sucked in a breath from a twinge of pain. "Easy, breathe slowly. Relax." Once the pain eased and he was moving his fingers freely, he removed them, then picked up a butt plug from the table and coated it with lubricant. "This will help you open some more for me." He eased the plug in and moved it around, in and out. "Good, slave."

"Master, that feels good. Please, fuck me. I need your cock now."

"Not yet, trust me to decide when. I want to make sure you're ready."

Finally, he took the butt plug out and added a heavy amount of lubricant to his condom. "I'm going to fuck your ass, Dana. Slow, easy now."

"Yes, yes."

He eased in, inch by inch, giving her time to become accustomed to his size. "Damn, your ass is so tight."

"Take me now, please."

He groaned and sank into her. She gasped, but he wasn't in her all the way. Holding back must be pure torture. He stilled. Was he trying to keep from hurting her or coming?

He glanced at her and the dark look he gave her was so full of love and lust. Her heart soared. The final surrender. "Fuck me, Master. Deep, all the way."

She sucked in a ragged breath as his hand stroked her clit. Shattering into a fierce orgasm, she cried out as the sensations coursed through her body. The climax was so intense, almost unbearable. "Never been so good," she murmured. Afterward, she hung limp in the restraints.

"My pleasure." He closed his eyes and thrust into her ass the rest of the way, then held still as her body accepted all of him. He was so hard and thick, and his slow, easy strokes gradually increased and drew the most exquisite pleasure. Tugging against her restraints, she raised her hips slightly, urging him deeper.

The muscles in his face, his arms and chest were rigid and coated with a thin sheen of sweat. Her muscles strained against the restraints, but she found the complete loss of control, and giving her power up to him, elicited the most delicious sensations and joy. "Master, yes," she breathed and wriggled her ass. The movement sent him over the edge. He sucked in a breath and groaned as he reached his climax.

Gripping her buttocks, he held tight until the aftershocks subsided. He slipped from her body, unfastened the straps and helped her down. For a long moment he held her close. She didn't want to let go. She didn't want to think about tomorrow, the weeks after and the decisions she had to make.

After they cleaned up, he lifted her in his arms and sat her down on the bed. "Let's remove these." She cried out in pain as he released the clamps and tossed them on a side table. "How are you doing?" He brushed her hair back from her face and kissed her forehead.

"Drained but wonderful," she said, smiling.

He chuckled. "Hmmm. I figured that." He gave her a long, loving look that made her heart break. "I also understand why you craved the pain."

"Why?"

He laughed. "Don't you know?"

She thought for a moment. "When I watched Shannon and Damon that first time, she appeared to experience extreme pain but also exquisite pleasure. I wanted to feel that."

"She had reached subspace, a trance-like state brought on by an intense experience, and can give an out-of-body sensation. You were there yourself tonight, at least the beginning. It's more than that."

"I did feel as though I were floating."

"You don't need to experience extreme pain to reach that state, just an intense session, complete surrender," Jack added.

She laughed. "We'll have to try different things to see what I do like. Why else do you think I craved the pain?"

"The physical pain helps you avoid the emotional pain that's coming."

"Maybe."

"Only endure the pain if you enjoy it."

"Exactly."

He hugged her close. "Are you ready to go home?"

"Home?" She groaned. "I don't want to think about that. I haven't decided yet."

Jack smiled and tapped her nose with his finger. "I meant have you had enough of Dagda's Edge for tonight? Would you like to go back to your cottage?"

"Oh yes. I'd like to go back now."

"Dana, I love you, and you know I want you to stay in Ireland. But I'll understand if you have to go."

"I know, Jack."

CHAPTER EIGHTEEN

A Ghost?

She awoke in her bed to the sound of birds chirping outside and sunlight streaming into her cottage. She reached to the other side of the bed and it was empty. "Jack?" There was no movement in the bathroom and she didn't see any of his clothes on the floor. Had he gotten up and left without waking her?

She stood and looked around for a note or something but didn't see anything. It was still early. Maybe he went into town to work at the store. After showering and getting dressed she strolled outside to a warm August morning. She checked his cottage and he wasn't there. He must be in town.

As early as it was, no other cars were parked in front of the other entertainers' cottages. They must all be early risers and had gone into town to shop. She gazed into the forest where Shannon had taken her to Dagda's Edge last night. The trail was still there. It wouldn't be hard to find now in the daylight. Curiosity drove her to explore the forest. The perfect day for it, and she wanted to see Dagda's Edge in the daylight. The walk should only take about fifteen minutes if she remembered correctly.

Dana entered the forest and followed the trail. High grass and low-hanging tree branches covered most of the narrow path. Thankfully, Shannon had shown her the way last night; otherwise she didn't think she could've found her way in the dark.

Even in the daylight, she expected to see the cottage by now. The forest was very disorienting. When she came upon a set of stone pillars, at first she thought she'd found a different gate, possibly turned down a fork in the trail, because there was no house.

But the pillars had the same wrought-iron gate with a bent Celtic motif. This was the right place.

She screamed. An icy terror gripped her as she stared at the bare overgrown space of grass and tall weeds. The cottage was gone! It hadn't been but twenty or thirty yards from the gate and now there was nothing. The building had vanished, and there was no sign that anything had ever been there.

Had she been hallucinating? Dreaming? Did the previous night of lovemaking with Jack really happen? And Shannon and the others at Dagda's Edge, were they real or imagined? Her body shook so badly she grasped the gate to steady herself. She could accept the magic and mystery of an old brooch, even though she didn't understand it, and accept the possibilities of earth energies from ley lines. Weren't many stone circles build on ley lines and said to have supernatural powers? But a house that vanishes? She had to find Jack. Find out what was happening. What if Jack was gone too, like the cottage?

She raced back toward the castle and the cottages. Dana knocked on Jack's door and when he didn't answer she tried Kevin's and Thea's, Damon's and Shannon's. No one was around. She could drive to his uncle's shop. What if she'd imagined Jack and the others too?

Covering her face with her hands, she ran to the castle and it was closed. Checking her watch, she noticed it was too early for visitors. What if she was the key that allowed them to return to another place and time? Jack had said the brooch was an invitation, a key.

A crushing weight slammed into her chest. Jack, where are you? What if he'd been a ghost all along? What if they all were? She looked at the ancient castle. A five-hundred-year-old fortress must have many ghosts. Had she lost Jack for good?

Her hand went to her mouth to smother a sob. My God, she was losing it. None of this could be true. She loved Jack. Yes, she was sure of that now. He was her Master. And given the chance she would stay in Ireland with him and not go back to her old job. She could visit her friends and family or they could come to see her. Why had she been struggling with that decision? It was so clear to her now. But it was too late if Jack was a ghost or gone to another dimension. He was lost to her forever. Tears filled her eyes and spilled onto her cheeks.

She barely registered the sound of footsteps on the gravel walkway. "Morning, my lady, have you had breakfast?"

"Jack!" She ran over and into his arms. Tears spilled down her cheeks.

"Hey, hey, what's wrong? You're crying." He lifted her chin and studied her through narrow eyes.

"I woke up and you were gone."

"Sorry, I promised Donegal to help move some furniture this morning. I figured I'd be back before you woke up. It took longer than I expected."

Taking her by the shoulders, he held her back. "What else is going on? You're shaking."

"I took a walk into the forest."

Jack groaned.

Dana ignored him and continued. "I followed the trail to Dagda's Edge and it's gone. I found the gate where Shannon took me through, but the building is completely gone."

Jack nodded. "Yeah, it does that."

She looked at him strangely, but then it seemed to make sense. "Will it come back?"

Jack shrugged. "It does, when the energy is aligned. I don't quite understand it." He pulled her into his arms. "Want to tell me why you were crying?"

"I thought I lost you. I thought everyone had left with the cottage. All this mystical stuff is making me crazy."

"Understandable. It takes a while to get used to." He stroked her hair. "The others went into town to visit Jane. She had her babe."

Dana laughed. "I'm not crazy then?"

"No, there are many unexplained things here at Rathmore Castle."

"And what is this brooch all about? I still don't understand why Dru gave it to me."

"It's a gift and invitation. When you arrived, she sensed you belonged here, and believes you had been a guest from another time."

"I don't understand."

"Cleona and Adara were friends from the 15th Century. Adara was betrothed to a man she didn't love. Cleona was in a dangerous love triangle. Cleona and Adara escaped their time through Dagda's Edge. But Cleona wanted to return, even as a secret mistress. Her guilt and love for the earl was stronger than her love for me. The brooch was a gift from her lover, and she left it behind, perhaps by accident. Adara said she was murdered in the bog by guards of the castle. She thinks the earl's wife discovered her. Dru and Adara think you're Cleona reborn."

"Reincarnated? Your lover? Do I look like her?"

"Not at all, and you don't act like her. You described how she died in your dreams, but you may have psychically picked up on that energy. It doesn't mean you are Cleona."

"Still, I found my way here by many synchronistic events. I don't know if I am and it doesn't matter. But I have made a decision about what I'm doing at the end of the summer."

He didn't give her a chance to finish. "I've been thinking too. I could make arrangements for my uncle. If we sell his shop, I could have it written in the contract that my uncle would be kept on as an employee, for a set number of years."

"No, that's your family's shop. Don't sell it."

"I can't bear to see you return to the states without me, so if you'll have me, I'll return with you. Just give me some time to settle things with the shop." He took her face in his hands and focused his gaze into her eyes. "I love you, Dana, I want us to be together."

"No, don't."

Jack stood back and fell silent. The hurt look on his face shredded her and she wanted to cry. "Aww, Dana, I feel like a jerk. I thought you'd be happy. I misread you."

"No, Jack, you didn't. Don't sell the shop. I'm staying here with you. I love you. Although it scares the hell out me having to depend on you for a while until I can find work, I can't imagine leaving you. This is where I belong. The security job may pay well but it doesn't give me joy. You were right. Playing my harp gives me joy. Loving you gives me joy. Being your sex slave gives me joy."

Jack smiled, pulled her into his arms and kissed her hard on the mouth before setting her down again. "I love you, Dana. I need you in my life, and I want you as my submissive for as long as you want me as your Master." He looked at the sky and laughed. "And nothing mystical or supernatural will take you away from me."

"Yes, I'm ready for whatever you have in mind, Master," she teased.

He growled. "Hmmm. Be careful, remember I own a store full of bondage devices."

"Now you're teasing me." Her pussy clenched thinking about the new things he would try with her.

"Go back to your cottage, strip and wait on the bed. I'll come down and teach you a few things about knots and ropes, then feed you breakfast while you're bound."

"I'll be eagerly waiting."

Rathmore Tower

As the guests from the dinner show began to file out of the castle on the night of her last performance, she noticed Jack talking to a few of the entertainers. She hoped to see him later tonight to discuss her plans for moving out of her cottage and into his apartment close to the store. Although depending on Jack for a job and a home wasn't ideal, he insisted she would soon find employment either with her harp or in the security business. She was following her heart, trusting him and their love, even though she felt like she was jumping out of an airplane without a parachute and expecting the ground to provide a soft landing.

Jack's Uncle Lee had been in the audience that evening and after the show he came up to her. "Glory, Dana, you do play the folk harp beautifully."

"Thank you, Mr. Keagan."

"Call me Lee. And can you forgive an old goat for being harsh with you?"

Dana smiled. "Of course, it's all right."

He gave her a kiss on the cheek. "I'm pleased you'll be staying," he declared. "In truth, I've not seen my nephew this happy in a long time."

Dana pressed her hand to her heart. "Thanks for saying so."

"I'll see you at the store. Good night." After a few words with his nephew, he left the great hall.

While she waited for Jack, she strummed out an old folk song Kevin was teaching her. Mr. Donegal walked over to her. "Lovely performance, Dana, a gift you have there," Mr. Donegal said, admiring her instrument. "Like listening to an angel play."

"Thank you. Your other harpist, Jane, should be back this week."

"Wanted to talk to you about that now." He scratched his chin. "Jane has decided to stay home with her babe. She won't be coming back to Rathmoor Castle. She'll fill in as needed but I'd hoped you'd considering staying on with us."

"Really?" Her fingers gripped her harp so hard she thought she'd leave permanent dents. Glancing around the room, she looked for Jack. He'd be thrilled. Jack strolled out of the hall with a group of guests and entertainers, taking the stone stairway to the lower level.

She'd have to talk to him later. "Thanks, Mr. Donegal, I'd love to."

He asked her to stop by the office the next day to make arrangements then left the hall. Shannon came over. "You're all smiles, Dana."

"Jane has decided not to come back to the show, and Mr. Donegal asked me to stay and replace her."

"And you agreed."

Dana nodded.

"Wonderful. I'm sure Jack will be pleased. Does he know yet?"

"No, could you tell him to meet me on top of the castle? I want to surprise him."

"Sure thing. So glad you're staying with us. I was going to miss you terribly in the show," Shannon said, giving her a hug.

* * *

Standing on top of the ancient castle, she looked out at the glow of lights from the cottages. A warm breeze swayed the pine trees. And the sounds of night creatures drifted up from the forest and bog. The sky was clear except for a few clouds. Were lights flickering deep within the trees, had Dagda's Edge returned, or was it reflections in the bogs?

Dana wondered how many lovers over the centuries had stood looking out from that turret, a lord and lady, a crusader and maiden, arguing over some impediment, or making romantic plans for their future. Jack was in love with her. And she was in love with him. That was all that mattered.

This would be her new home. The excitement and anticipation tingled through her. Yes, this was where she belonged. The door to the roof creaked open and Jack stepped out.

"Shannon said you had some news." He took her in his arms and kissed her.

"Jane isn't coming back. Mr. Donegal asked me to stay on. So you don't have to put me up in your apartment if you don't want to. I can stay in the cottage."

"I love you, Dana. I want us to be together as lovers and friends, as Master and slave." He hugged her then squeezed her breasts through the thick fabric of the costume. Her body heated. She wanted him right there, right now on top of the castle. Gripping the material of his medieval tunic, she pulled him closer. Time seemed to stand still for a moment. Looking into his eyes, she saw lust and also love. How could she have considered leaving him?

"Would you rather stay in the cottage or at the store?" His face was emotionless but intense.

She chuckled. "I'll stay with you."

"Great. You can still work in the store if you like. I'll give my uncle a good talking to. I'm sure over time he'll get to love you. He's cautious about people and remembers how a woman broke my heart years ago."

"I think we'll get along fine," she said.

He hugged her again. "I'm so glad you're staying with the troupe. When did Donegal give you the news?"

"Right after the show."

"And you didn't come to tell me straight away? I might have to punish you for that," he teased.

"Please, Master, please." Turning around, she bent over the wall, facing out toward the forest where the mysterious cottage had once been. Where she had learned about glorious surrender. "Wait. Those are lights in the forest, not a reflection. Has Dagda's Edge reappeared do you think?"

"Possibly. Shannon would know. She has a sense of it when it returns." He gently pressed her shoulders toward the low wall. "Let's see what you have under your skirt, my lady."

She flipped the hem of her dress up and stuck out her naked bottom to him. "My lord, I'm ready for my punishment."

"No panties? Hmmm." His hand rubbed the bare skin of her ass. "My lady, I do believe a most severe punishment is in order."

Below the castle, figures dressed in black robes approached the forest. "They must see the lights too," Dana exclaimed.

"Ah, you were right. Would you like to continue your punishment here or at Dagda's Edge?" He took her arm and pulled her into an embrace.

"I'd like to see the cottage again. Adara said she wanted to tell me about her past. I'd like to hear her story of how she came to Dagda's Edge. I think we'll be good friends."

"I think you're right." He took her hand and led her down the stone staircase. "Those who come to Dagda's Edge are drawn there for a reason. We found what we needed there."

THE END

ABOUT KATHY

New York Times & *USA Today* bestselling author Kathy Kulig is known for her sexy paranormal and contemporary romances that are passionate, intense and riveting. These emotionally-charged stories are full of heart and always have a happy ending.

She began her writing career in journalism, publishing articles in magazines and newspapers. Kathy has been featured or quoted in the *Chicago Tribune*, *Writer's Digest*, *Romantic Times Magazine*, *USA Today HEA*, *Bustle Magazine*, *Florida Weekly*, and appeared on several radio shows. She has spoken at national and local conferences, writer's groups and libraries.

When she's not writing, she loves to work out, travel, read good books, watch movies and have dinners out with her darling husband. She lives in Pennsylvania in a 100-year-old Victorian house with a garage built out of reject tombstones.

Connect with Kathy on her website: www.kathykulig.com. Subscribe to her newsletter so you don't miss a thing! Read more about Kathy, her books, contest and upcoming projects by subscribing to her mailing list.

http://smarturl.it/KathysHotNews.

Web site: http://www.kathykulig.com

Blog: http://www.BurntStilettos.com

Facebook: http://www.facebook.com/kathykuligauthor

Twitter: http://www.twitter.com/kathykulig

Goodreads:

https://www.goodreads.com/author/show/1221829.Kathy
_Kulig

Hot News Mailing List:

http://smarturl.it/KathysHotNews

A Note from the Author

THANK YOU FOR READING!

I hope you enjoyed reading this book as much as I enjoyed writing it. Several years ago, I traveled to Ireland and visited the Bunratty Castle, a 15th Century castle with medieval dinner show. I loved Ireland, the people and the country. The beautiful setting of this castle sparked an idea for the book. I wanted it to have an enchanted, mystical, or supernatural theme, as well as romantic and sexy.

I grew up reading science fiction and paranormal books, and watching television shows like Twilight Zone, Outer Limits and Night Gallery. Okay, I may be dating myself, but I loved these series, and my bookshelves started filling up with supernatural books at an early age.

These shows featured thought–provoking dark fantasy, science fiction and supernatural stories. All were stand alone. By the way, Night Gallery featured the directorial debut Steven Spielberg!

ABOUT DARK REALMS SERIES

Influenced by these television shows, and my love for paranormal and speculative fiction, I've created the Dark Realms series. It's is a collection of sensual romance novellas and short novels with supernatural heroes and fantasy, science fiction or paranormal elements. Shifters, witches, vampires, ghosts and more. These stories can be set on Earth, on other planets, within another dimension or time. You'll find supernatural heroes who haunt us, hunt us and hunger passionately for us. Each book is a complete and individual story. No cliffhangers!

The books can be read in any order.

Reviews are helpful to authors. I really appreciate all reviews, both positive and negative. If you want to leave one, please do so on Goodreads or your favorite retailer! If you liked this story, you might also enjoy other books in the Dark Realms series as well as other books by Kathy Kulig.

Preview
Tattoo Witch

CHAPTER ONE

"Sam, stop. People will see us." Anita shoved his chest.

"It was only a kiss," Sam teased.

"Yeah, sure. You grabbed my breasts." She rushed past him, heading toward the beach that overlooked the bay of Ocean City, Maryland. Moonlight glistened on the water and an offshore breeze thrashed at the palm fronds. Maybe he was pushing too hard. This vacation was supposed to stir up a little excitement in their life, especially their sex life. He didn't need to pressure her.

His girlfriend stood at the shoreline, her arms wrapped tightly around her waist. She swayed to the reggae music playing in the background. Annoyed, but not angry. A year together and he still couldn't keep his eyes or hands off her. The wind whipped strands of her long, brown hair against high cheekbones, a petite nose and dimpled chin. Anita always complained that her jawline was too angular, but Sam said it gave her a sexy, brainy look. He was pretty certain she wore the tight skirt for him. She knew it was his favorite. When they first met, he was entranced by her eyes, not her curvy ass. Behind that gaze, he'd sensed an intelligent, kind and affectionate person. Then he'd noticed her hot ass. Many times she flashed those sultry, hazel eyes, trying to work him around her finger. He even played along on occasion.

"Ouch!" Anita hopped on one foot as she kicked off her shoe. "I stepped on a shell or something."

"Hold onto me." Sam brushed off her sandal and foot, then slipped the sandal back on. "Better?"

She nodded. Hooking her arms around his neck, she kissed him. Her low–cut tank offered a glimpse of cleavage.

Most of the clientele from Seacrets, the outdoor bar, restaurant and nightclub, were dancing near the band or seated at tables eating dinner. No one was by the beach area. "I thought it'd be romantic here," he explained, trying to keep his voice light as he stared out over the water.

Several round floats, the size of small mattresses, bobbed in the water. Unlike daytime, the beachside bar was closed. The boat dock, deserted. She gave him that don't-bull-shit-me look. He knew what that meant. They'd been together long enough for him to know all her expressions and moods. "You wanted to fool around," she said.

"What's wrong with that?"

She frowned, then finally smiled and slipped her arm around him, giving in a little. "Nothing. But I don't care to get groped in public."

"I didn't grope you," he argued.

"You grabbed my breasts."

"I was checking to see if you wore a bra tonight."

"Right." She huffed. "I always wear a bra."

"I know, just fantasizing."

She leaned into him. "I love fooling around with you. We can fool around when we get back to the hotel."

If he kept arguing, he wouldn't get any tonight. "Okay. Ready for a drink?"

"Shhhh." Anita's eyes widened and gripped his arm.

Sam felt his cock grow hard. "Change your mind?"

"No, be quiet. Look, on the raft."

"Where?"

"By the boat dock. The last one in the back row," she whispered.

Lights from the dock shone on a naked couple lying on one of the rafts and fucking like porn stars. "Cool. At least someone's getting lucky."

Anita punched him in the arm…hard.

"Ow."

"Let's go," she whispered.

"No, let's watch. If we leave now, they'll know we saw them." A lame excuse, but the only one he could come up with at the moment.

"So? They obviously don't care." Anita strained for a closer look. "What's he wearing? Does he have a shirt on?"

Sam tried to make out the man who was pumping his cock into his woman and somehow managing to keep from tipping the raft over. "No, I think he has tattoos, a lot of them. He's got great balance. With all that thrusting how does he manage not to flip the raft?"

"It is pretty hot to watch," Anita said with a raspy voice.

"Yeah." Was she getting turned on? How cool would that be? With his hand on her waist, Sam slid upward and grazed the underside of her breast. He was rewarded with her sharp intake of breath. Encouraged, he let his hand slide down and underneath her shirt. This time when he grasped her breast, she didn't protest. Hallelujah.

"Feels good," she whispered, leaning into him. Her full lips glistened, begging to be kissed. He took the chance and lowered his mouth to her lips. She pressed a hand to his chest. "Stop. Look, they've finished anyway." The couple had climbed up on the boat dock and got dressed.

Disappointed, Sam took his hand out from under Anita's shirt. His cock was still freaking hard.

"I'm ready for that drink," she said.

"Right," he muttered.

They ordered drinks from an outside bar that was built to look like an old shipwrecked boat. Sam took a swig from his beer and Anita sipped on her rum punch. "There they are." He tilted his head as the exhibitionists approached the bar. The woman had on a low-cut top that showed off a decent set of breasts and several tats on her arms, shoulders and chest. He wondered how far down the ink went. No doubt the design circled each breast. His cock came to life again. Hey, he was a guy after all.

Her short red hair was damp from their evening swim. Her man was well built, about the same height as Sam, with sandy colored hair that came down past his shoulders. He wore a black Harley tee with the sleeves cut out. Both arms were covered in tats. His neck had a coiled snake or a dragon design. The tattooed man and woman sat next to Sam and Anita. Sam noticed the wedding bands.

Anita vigorously stirred the bottom of her drink while sucking on the straw and slurping the last of the frozen concoction.

"I think your lady is ready for another drink," tattooed guy said with a friendly tone. "Mind if my wife and I buy you two a drink?"

Anita stopped slurping and gave Sam a warning look. He loved his girlfriend dearly, but wished she wasn't quite so conservative. This couple was just being friendly. But why did they decide to sit next to him and Anita?

Stop assuming the worst. Sam Quinn was used to expecting the worst in people—a side effect from working airport security. Terrorists at Seacrets were likely a low-risk concern. Perhaps this couple did have ulterior motives, like wife swapping. That wasn't exactly Sam's kink, but it didn't mean he couldn't have some fun chatting with them. "A drink? That's nice of you to offer," Sam said. "You don't have to—"

"It's our pleasure," the woman added. "I'm Rene and this is my husband, Perry. We're from Baltimore." She rested her hands on the bar. On the back of Rene's hand was a detailed rose tat. It looked 3D. Ink designs covered Perry's hands too.

Sam introduced himself and Anita. Anita gave him a kick. He was going to get hell later, but the intricate detail of Rene's tattoo was mesmerizing.

"Have you tried Swamp Water?" Perry asked Anita.

She looked confused.

"They're good. They're coconut rum, pineapple juice and Curaçao. Try one," Rene said as she waved to the bartender and ordered two and a couple beers.

"We were about to leave, right Sam?" Anita shot him a look.

"Oh, you can hang for a drink," Rene said. "It's still early."

Anita scowled at her murky green drink when it arrived but didn't argue with Rene. Taking a sip, she smiled. "Mmmm. It is good."

"What kind of work do you do, Sam?" Perry asked.

"TSA agent."

"Interesting." Perry locked his gaze with him. Red flags waved in the back of Sam's mind.

As a TSA agent, Sam had an uncanny gift of reading people's eyes, expressions and body language. Something in Perry's gaze alarmed him. If someone had looked at him like that while going through his TSA check point, he would give them a pat down. What were his eyes telling him? A warning? Fear? A challenge or threat? Sam couldn't figure it out. Something wasn't right about these two. Or maybe he needed this vacation more than he thought.

"I've been admiring your tattoos," Sam said as he watched their expressions. "Excellent work. It must've taken a long time to have those done. Were they all by the same artist?"

Perry and Rene exchanged a look. "Yes, she's local," Perry said. "On the boardwalk."

"I don't remember a tattoo parlor and we come here often." Anita had sucked down half her drink. "What do you have on your neck?" she asked Perry.

Perry got up and sat on the stool next to her. Turning his head to the side, he elongated his neck, offering Anita a better view. "What would you call it?"

"It's a dragon. A magnificent dragon. Look at all the colors." While Perry pointed out his various tattoos, Rene showed the vine of roses coiling up her arm.

"Do the tats have specific meanings or stories?" Sam asked. "They're very detailed."

She laughed out loud. "Sort of."

He noticed a shadow of sadness drift across Rene's face. Anita was oblivious to his conversation. The designs on the man's forearms enthralled her. She was literally staring. Fuck.

"Do you think tattoos are sexy?" Rene asked seductively.

"I guess." He forced himself not to look at her deep cleavage and the tats that decorated her skin there. Man, he needed to take Anita back to the hotel and fuck her brains out before she got wasted on Swamp Water.

"How about mine?" Rene ran her hands over her arms, then stroked the tops of her breasts.

"Yes, I'd say so," Sam replied. Holy shit, she was flirting with him. "There." Rene eased the sleeve of Sam's tee shirt up over his shoulder. "You have nice biceps and shoulders. The perfect place for tats." Her fingernail drew imaginary designs on his arm.

He studied her with the narrowed gaze he reserved for troublemakers at the airport and added a cocky smile. "Think so?"

"Yes," she breathed, leaning closer. "Men also look hot with tats on their calves and thighs. Her hand dropped to his knee, just below his cargo shorts. Would she slide those up too? His cock stirred. How much had she drunk?

Anita laughed. Sam glanced at Perry flexing his arm, making a scorpion tat appear to crawl. His girlfriend was amused.

"Have you ever thought about getting a tat?" Rene asked Sam with a sultry, teasing tone. "Or maybe you have one hidden?" She removed her hand from his knee. Sam released his breath. "No. I've thought about getting one. But I don't have any." Damn, it was getting warm. Was Rene coming on to him with her husband right there? He glanced back at Anita again. She was having another Swamp Water. Terrific.

"You should get one. You and your lady," Rene said. "We get ours at Sinful Designs on the boardwalk. They do the best work."

Ah, now he got it. "I suppose you two work there? Or own the business."

She laughed. "You think we're trying to drum up sales?"

Sam nodded.

"No, nothing like that. But there is something special about Sinful Designs that you won't find at any other tattoo parlor."

"Is that right?" Sam called over the bartender and ordered another beer and a drink for Rene. "Don't take this the wrong way but are you two hitting on us?"

"Not exactly," Perry said, looking up from his show-and-tell for Anita. "We saw you watching us earlier—"

"And you thought we'd like to hook up with you two," Sam finished the sentence, sounding slightly annoyed but intrigued.

"That's not it," Rene said. "But I bet you wished you were out there having the most amazing sex with Anita. Am I right?"

"Sure," Sam said.

Anita smiled nervously, then sipped more of her drink.

"What if I told you there was a way to increase your sexual enjoyment by at least ten times, be more adventurous, have longer hard-ons, and multiple orgasms?" Rene looked at Anita. "Anita, wouldn't you love to have multiple orgasms whenever you willed them to happen?"

Anita rolled her eyes. "I have orgasms."

"Four or five in one night, without being touched?"

"I'd say you're full of shit," Anita said.

Sam nearly choked on his beer. Anita Brooke never swore in front of strangers. She was getting drunk. Damn, he wasn't getting any tonight.

"Do you believe in magic, the supernatural?"

"I try to keep an open mind." Sam didn't want to discount anything. But more than that, he wanted to see where this was going.

"Try one of these tattoos at Sinful Designs. Just one. I promise you won't be disappointed." Rene paused. "Don't be surprised if you go back for more like we did." Eyes wide, she glanced around the night club's grounds, looked over her shoulder, then forced a smile. There was no hiding that look of terror. Cold fear flashed across her eyes. What had her so afraid? She didn't look the type to scare easily. A shiver slid down Sam's spine.

"Sounds too good to be true," Sam said as he briefly fantasized a few possibilities—sex on the raft, sex with this couple, and a few positions Anita wasn't crazy about trying. His cock throbbed as his heart pounded in his chest. The woman didn't look like she was lying. Was business that bad that this tattoo parlor would think up this fantastical story to bring in a few customers?

Rene placed a hand on his arm. "Honest, Sam, we don't make out financially if you get a tattoo. We're just amazed by this woman. She's a witch you know. Her name is Cassandra."

"A witch?" Anita asked.

Rene smiled at Sam. "Trust me. You will have the most scorching sex you could ever imagine."

End of preview for Tattoo Witch, Book 3.

Like to continue reading this book? Visit the author's website or find links at your favorite retailer.

http://www.kathykulig.com/books.html